AP

Halfway to Ventura I wanted to leave Nicole's sister by the side of the road.

She was whining, "Gracie Lee, Mom, this is so stupid. You know it's not going to be her. They said they found this girl naked washed up on the beach. That is so not anything Nicole would do."

"Paige, shut up," her mother finally snapped. "The goal of this trip is to make sure it isn't Nicole. And we all know it wouldn't be like her to go skinny-dipping in the ocean in June. Nobody in their right mind would do that."

Beside me in the front passenger seat, Hal gripped the armrest so tightly I was afraid it might come off in his hand. I almost felt like reaching over and patting his hand.

Regardless of who was there at the morgue to be identified, this would be a rough night for everyone involved.

Books by Lynn Bulock

Love Inspired Suspense

Where Truth Lies #56
No Love Lost #59

Love Inspired

Gifts of Grace #80
Looking for Miracles #97
Walls of Jericho #125
The Prodigal's Return #144
Change of the Heart #181
The Harbor of His Arms #204
Protecting Holly #279

Steeple Hill Single Title

Love the Sinner
Less Than Frank

LYNN BULOCK

has been writing since fourth grade and has been a published author in various fields for over twenty years. Her first romantic novel came out in 1989 and has been followed by more than twenty books since then. She lives near Los Angeles, California, with her husband. They have two grown sons.

LYNN BULOCK

No Love Lost

Published by Steeple Hill Books™

STEEPLE HILL BOOKS

ISBN-13: 978-0-373-44249-2
ISBN-10: 0-373-44249-1

NO LOVE LOST

This edition published by arrangement with Steeple Hill Books.

www.SteepleHill.com

Printed in U.S.A.

Love does not delight in evil but rejoices
with the truth. It always protects, always trusts,
always hopes, and always perseveres.

—*1 Corinthians* 13:6–7

To Joe, Always

And to two of the real-life couples who've shown me what marriage should be,

Jack and Bonnie David

Elton and Edna Peterson

Acknowledgments

Those who read my books know that the real Ventura County and Gracie Lee's version are a little different. I have taken literary license with quite a few things including geography, county government and structure of the Ventura County Sheriff's Department. Any errors are totally of my own making, and I am indebted to more people than I can mention who keep me from making more errors than I do. Special thanks to Linda Fisherman M.A., M.F.T., Sgt. Patti Salas of the Ventura County Sheriff's Department and Dr. Robert Hoffmann for their professional advice.

ONE

My ex-husband stood in the courtyard of his luxurious house, looking as agitated as I'd ever seen him. "Surely you realize that all of this is your fault," he said with a glare in my direction.

"Wow, what a big surprise. Twenty years later, a whole different wedding and Hal Harris is still totally blameless for any crisis that arises." Okay, so that wasn't very mature. But I couldn't find my son, my ex-husband was marrying a teenager he'd lost track of and perhaps I was under just a little more stress than usual. I'd work on mature later.

My name is Gracie Lee Harris. I'm a thirty-nine-year-old single mom, divorced—once—and widowed—once—still getting used to the fact that after a lifetime in Missouri I picked up and moved to Southern California about two years ago. Life has never been the same, but usually I mean that in a good way. Today I wasn't so sure.

I moved out here to follow my charming new second husband Dennis Peete. In a supreme act of love I even moved in with my mother-in-law, but that soon became the least of my problems. Dennis had a nasty car accident and an even nastier turn of events led to his murder, with the police suspecting me of the crime for a while.

The best thing about my move to California has been the wonderful group of women who have become my friends at the Conejo Community Chapel here in Rancho Conejo. The Christian Friends group has kept me together through two murder investigations, not to mention sane and striving toward a faith that would normally keep me from mouthing off, even to my ex-husband.

I'd married Hal Harris at nineteen, and we'd divorced before I was twenty-three. Our early shared history is probably one of the reasons that he can bring out the worst in me quicker than almost any person on the planet.

And of course today he'd done it again. I was fuming because he seemed to care a lot more that his fiancée Nicole was not where she should have been than he was about our son, Ben, being totally out of contact with both of his parents.

I exaggerated before about Nicole being a teenager. She is almost thirty, but looks younger than Ben does at nearly nineteen. She definitely doesn't look any older than Ben's girlfriend Cai Li who's just finished up her sophomore year at Pacific Oaks Christian College. Of course that may be because Nicole is so tiny she always looks like she's playing dress-up in her white medical coat over her size-0 wardrobe.

Tiny or not, I'd still argue that she's a grown-up and can take care of herself, whereas Ben is still navigating those waters into adulthood and far more likely to be in trouble. If he'd been at school I never would have known he hadn't come home the night before and I wouldn't be in such a panic. Instead, he'd come back to my apartment two days earlier when the semester ended. So it came as a shock on Saturday morning when his bedroom door was open and his bed still made.

"You're just overreacting," Hal said loudly, bringing me back to the present. "How do you know that Ben didn't come in after you went to bed, sleep a few hours and is already up and gone this morning?"

"He made no other mess in his room, made the bed and is gone before 8:00 a.m. on a Saturday? It would never happen." I was surprised Hal could even suggest it. "Of course I might say about the same regarding Nicole."

"No, you couldn't. At least her car is here." Hal motioned toward a small silver sedan that looked quite new and shiny. Probably a wedding present from my husband's part of the family business selling security systems. Or maybe it was a gift from one of Nicole's parents. I'd heard from Ben they competed for her loyalties as fiercely as Hal's mother and father did for my son's favor. In any case I was pretty sure that a doctoral student in psychology hadn't just gone out and bought a brand-new car.

"So her car is here but she isn't? Are you sure she didn't just go for a walk or something? I mean, surely you've talked to her in the last twelve hours?" *Unlike Ben,* I felt like adding. "And how on earth is any of this my fault?"

"That's two questions. Do you want me to answer either of them?" Hal ran a hand through his dark blond hair, only a couple of shades darker than Ben's and almost as long. I wondered if he was coloring it. Surely at forty he should have a little bit of gray, shouldn't he? Or had he left that all to me, along with the raising of our son?

"Second one first, I guess. I can understand how you'd blame me for Ben being gone, but Nicole? I don't follow your logic on that one."

"Aw, Gracie Lee, lighten up. On both of us, okay? Ben's a normal college kid with a girlfriend. There are half a dozen things he might be doing that would keep him out all night at his age. He's a little old to always be checking in with Mommy."

I wasn't going to give in on that point, because I knew Ben didn't drink, didn't do drugs, didn't hang out with people who did and was dating a girl who was even more serious about her faith than he was. But pointing out any of this to Hal right now would just mean another explosion. "And Nicole?" I prompted. I wasn't ready to give up on that issue.

He sighed, and for a moment Hal looked forty. His shoulders slumped and he looked so much like Ben I had a momentary impulse to hug him. It passed quickly. "Nicole's usually good about keeping me informed about where she is. And she's been so uptight about running into you in public, because she thinks she has this image to live up to."

I decided not to point out to Hal that Nicole and I had met on a regular basis in the last three weeks. If she hadn't shared that information with him, I wasn't about to do it now. "So where do you think she is?"

"Honestly? I don't have a clue. She went out last night, some last fling with a couple of girlfriends, but neither of them is the wild type. She told me she was going to sleep on the couch when she got in because she didn't want to wake me in the middle of the night. So I haven't seen her since six yesterday evening. Still, her car is here and the couch looks disturbed. Besides, she wouldn't just flake out on me this morning of all times."

"What makes today more important?"

"Her mom and her sister Paige are coming in later today and planning to stay through the wedding. Nicole's been obsessing for a week over having things perfect when they show up."

That explained some of Hal's stress right there. Two weeks of in-laws before an event as big as a wedding would put anybody on edge. And I knew he loved this young woman…impossibly young in my estimation…that he was getting ready to marry. "Okay, so maybe you should just hang tight here and wait for Nicole to call you. I assume you've tried her cell?"

"It's off, dumps me right to voice mail. And I can't find a number for either of her girlfriends, either. Both are probably on her PDA but I feel funny using it."

Hmm. Age had changed Hal. Fifteen years ago he wouldn't have given a second thought to someone else's boundaries like that. Not when the someone else was his wife, or in this case fiancée. "Do you want any kinds of official checks run on her yet?"

He shook his head. "No, because if I did that and she is really only out taking a long walk to clear her head or something, she'd have a fit when she got home. Besides, I don't want you or your cop boyfriend to do me any favors."

"Ray isn't just a cop and he isn't my boyfriend," I snapped. Ray Fernandez was a Ventura County Sheriff's Department detective and our relationship, although cordial, wasn't getting serious any time soon. For one thing, neither of us had time for serious.

Most of my time is spent finishing up my master's degree in counseling at Pacific Oaks Christian College, or keeping track of Ben. Then there's working as a barista at the Coffee Corner on campus, keeping active with my Christian Friends group at Conejo Community Chapel here in Rancho Conejo, and if there's any time left over after everything else I work in an occasional date with Ray.

Of course he's even busier than I am, so those dates are few and far between. The department had gone through a budget crises like every other government agency in California, and his already-crowded life as a homicide detective had gotten even more convoluted by the creation of a major crimes unit. Ray now investigates serious crimes involving live people as well as dead ones, and there are far more of those crimes in the county to keep him busy. All this added up to way more than I wanted to explain to Hal.

My frustration level had reached the boiling point and Hal was still being as obnoxious as ever. "I think maybe it's better if I go back home and wait for Ben to call, and you wait for Nicole. Call me if you hear from either of them."

And with that I turned around and got into my car before I cried in front of my ex-husband or got into a screaming match with him. I was praying for a phone to ring, which I found ironic. It was a ringing phone three weeks ago that had led me into the mess I was in now.

A ringing phone at 5:00 a.m. is every mother's nightmare. When Ben is at school a predawn phone call jars me awake into full panic. When he's with me, I still startle awake then because my mom living alone in Missouri worries me almost as much as Ben.

I would still be back in Missouri close to her if it weren't for my decision three years ago to marry Dennis and follow him out here within twelve months of our marriage. Before we got a chance to celebrate our second anniversary I was a widow with no illusions and little money, but a whole lot more faith than I'd ever had before. And that's still about where things stand today.

The illusions are still gone, and so is most of the money. I lost track of thirty thousand dollars through Dennis making some shady business arrangements and then dying before I could sort out his affairs. An insurance policy finally paid off five thousand, but everything else is still tied up in a long and complicated legal battle involving his other heirs including a grandson he never really knew and a daughter by another woman.

But going into all that in detail would take more time than I can spare, so I'll leave it at that. So the phone jarring me out of sleep made me worry about Ben first and my mother second. Surprisingly, the voice on the other end wasn't connected to either of them. "Gracie Lee?" the shaky voice asked. "I know it's a terrible time to be calling but I need help and you were the first person I thought of."

I was touched that my friend Linnette Parks would think of me first when there are so many other people in her life that are more qualified to handle trouble. As a Christian Friends leader she's the person I would turn to in crisis myself. If she had a problem I would have thought she would call Pastor George from church, or somebody else with ministry training.

I've got little training in how to minister to others, but Linnette and some of the group say I've got a natural talent. I'm not sure how right they are, although I do know that people in virtually any situation feel free to come up to me in public and share their problems with me.

"What do you need help with?" At least I had my feet over the side of the bed and felt like I was semi-alert. Already my brain shouted that coffee and brushing my teeth would both be very good ideas before doing much else.

"I feel terrible, really down and scared. Could you come over and sit with me for a couple hours until my doctor's office opens?"

"Sure, unless you'd rather go to an emergency room," I offered.

Her answer was swift. "No, no emergency room. And don't call Ray, either."

"Don't worry, I hadn't planned to." Her response left me mystified but I had no intention to go against her wishes. I figure Linnette knows more about most things involving health and crisis than I do, unless the subject at hand is being under investigation for murder. On that subject I have more experience than she does, even though I hate to admit it.

I pushed a wave of honey-blond hair out of my face—it's actually Caramel Frappe, thanks to the same stylist who does Linnette's Vivacious Auburn—and contemplated how to manage things. Linnette sounded awfully shaky. Did I have time for a shower? I decided that was a bad idea and put on coffee to brew while I washed my face, brushed my teeth and slid into clothes. In about ten minutes I was out the door of the apartment. In fifteen more I was at Linnette's house, a tidy three-bedroom ranch style on one of the "tree streets" in Rancho Conejo.

Those streets were actually all called Calle, which means "street" in Spanish, followed by something descriptive like the name of a tree. The system always made me wish I'd taken more Spanish. Linnette's command of the language was about the best of anybody I knew from church. She said it was from living here so many years and wanting to talk to everybody. A transplanted Mid-westerner like me, she came for college and never moved back home. And now, a widow with two basically grown daughters, she wasn't likely to leave anytime soon.

Surprise bordering on shock hit me when she opened her front door. I'd never seen my friend look as worn or disheveled as she did now. My first thought was that something had happened to one of the girls, and I asked her. "No, they're both fine as far as I know," she said, voice dull. "It's just me."

We went back to the family room where one lone lamp burned in the predawn, casting a dim circle of light next to a worn recliner. The afghan draped over one arm told me that whatever sleep she'd gotten had probably been here. "I put on coffee after I called you. I can't vouch for it being any good, but it's black and hot."

"Then let me get us both a cup while you settle down there." I pointed to the recliner. "And then you can tell me what's going on." Everything I'd seen so far made me think of one answer. Linnette made no secret among the Christian Friends that she suffered from bouts of clinical depression. Most of the time medication, exercise and lots of prayer kept it in check. This morning those things didn't seem to be working.

While I poured coffee I tried to figure out why her condition felt like such a shock. We'd seen each other in passing at work, but with the end of the semester coming up fast our time to really talk was sharply curtailed. Add that to the fact that I'd been going to a different service at the chapel and it explained why Linnette's depression slid by me.

Putting on a more cheerful face, I came back with two steaming mugs. "We'll have to drink it black unless you have some creamer stashed someplace," I told her as matter-of-factly as I could.

She gave a mirthless little laugh. "The milk's sour, isn't it? I haven't been to the grocery store in a week or two."

"I noticed. What have you been eating?" Now that I looked at her, Linnette looked thinner than usual. Like me, she could usually stand to shed a few pounds, but now it appeared to be fewer than usual.

She shrugged in answer to my question. "Not enough of anything, I guess. I'm just not hungry most of the time."

"And you've been so busy at work, with the book buy-back for the end of the semester, and doing the ordering for next fall and setup for summer school that you haven't been exercising, either, have you?"

She shook her head and I noticed tears in her eyes. Everything together sounded a huge alarm for me. We'd talked about the signs and symptoms of depression in our Christian Friends meetings more than once. "Okay, how bad is it? You're not eating, not sleeping well and haven't been exercising."

Linnette looked down, picking at a fuzzy pill on the granny-square afghan. "It's bad, Gracie Lee." She was silent for a while and I didn't press her. She needed to get this out in her own time. "It's worse than it's ever been and it just crept up on me. I woke up about four thinking that it would be so nice if I could go back to sleep and not wake up again."

I felt as if someone had poured ice water through my insides. "Are you sure we shouldn't go to the emergency room?"

She looked up quickly. "Positive. I'll explain about that later. For now let's pray together and wait for the sun to come up. After that I'll put a call in to my doctor or whoever is on call for her, and we'll start putting me back together."

"We can start doing that right now," I told my best friend, grasping her cool fingers in my hands and scooting my chair closer to the recliner. I tried to keep my voice from betraying the fear I felt as I began praying out loud. Sunrise couldn't come soon enough.

TWO

By noon I'd driven Linnette to the offices of the counseling group she'd used in the past. Their attractive, calm, waiting room featured soothing music played over artfully hidden speakers and a tabletop fountain that burbled on a console in one corner. The music was nice, but I wondered about the fountain. Surely I wasn't the only person in the waiting room that had distracting physical symptoms with the sound of running water. We hadn't quite gotten settled yet before a pretty woman with silver hair came out and called her name.

"Aw, sweetie," she said, looking into Linnette's face as she rose from her seat. "Come back here and tell me what's going on." They disappeared into an office and I looked over the magazines on the coffee table. Unlike a lot of doctor's offices, these at least bore this year's date.

By the time Linnette came back forty-five

minutes later I had all kinds of great ideas on redecorating my apartment, none of which could be achieved on my budget. My current landlady was another Christian Friends member, Dot Morgan. The recent kitchen and bath remodel was functional and nice-looking, but it needed some touches to give it personality. Unfortunately most home magazine ideas would eat more paycheck than it took to feed the two of us for a month.

"I'll call you tonight. And again tomorrow morning, okay?" The woman I assumed was Linnette's doctor looked over rainbow-framed half-glasses waiting for an answer.

"All right. And I'll answer the phone, even if I don't want to," Linnette told her. She introduced me to the doctor and told her that I was the chauffeur for the time being.

"Great. It's good to know you've got a support system. You'll need it for a while."

Linnette's smile looked a little stronger. "I always need it. Thanks for being part of it." We left and she filled me in on what would happen next while we waited in the elevator lobby.

"First I hit the pharmacy, and then we go home so that I can make a couple phone calls. The good doctor wants me to be in counseling to go along with the medication, of course. And naturally my insurance won't pay for her rate because she's a psychiatrist. So she referred me to a therapy group for women run out of Playa del Sol."

"Where's that?" I knew the names of most of the local hospitals, and that wasn't one of them that I recognized.

"It's a private place halfway between here and Ventura. They have inpatient treatment for addiction problems and emotional illnesses. Fortunately they also have outpatient therapy, because that's all my budget can handle right now."

Once we got to the car Linnette thanked me again. "I'll pay for your gas while you ferry me all over the county," she said, getting in the passenger side of my compact.

"Don't worry about that now. Let's get you to the pharmacy and maybe swing by a grocery store to pick up a few things that might tempt you."

"That will be a challenge. Nothing sounds real good right now." She didn't have to tell me that, the way her clothes fit. Still, I knew it was important to get her to eat something.

It didn't work too well; she only picked at lunch when I fixed it. "I guess I ought to call the hospital to see how soon I can get into Ms. Barnes's therapy group. I'll still need a driver the first few times. Are you up for that or should I count on cabs?"

"You're joking, right? I'm up for that. I'm surprised you even had to ask."

She shrugged. "I can't make you do everything. Should I make it an evening group for your convenience, or morning?"

"Go for morning," I told her. Maria usually wanted me later in the day at the Coffee Corner. "What did you say the therapist's name was?"

"Nicole Barnes. Why?"

"It rings a bell, and I hope it isn't for the reason I think it is." While she went into the next room and made her phone call I pulled out my cell phone and made one of my own to Ben.

Fortunately my son was between classes and answered his phone. Cell phones with Caller ID make calls so much less of a surprise. "Hi, Mom. I've been meaning to call you," my offspring said in a tone that suggested something he didn't really want to discuss with me, at least on the phone.

For a change I decided not to push the issue. One crisis at a time is usually enough for me. "Hi, Ben. I've got a question for you. What is your dad's fiancée's full name?"

There was a pause. "I thought you didn't want to know anything more about her."

I still didn't, but life was forcing the issue. "I changed my mind."

Ben sighed. "Nicole Barnes. Does this mean you want to meet her, after all?" I'd resisted all attempts from Ben and his father to get to know my ex-husband's much younger fiancée since they moved to the area in February from Nashville, where Hal had lived since our divorce sixteen years ago. He'd been sweet-talked back home then by his mother, and he'd stayed in the area until this year, a move that had kind of blindsided me.

I hadn't figured Hal to be the type to fall for a graduate student at Vanderbilt more than a decade his junior but that wasn't the thing that surprised me the most. The fact that Nicole was his fiancée didn't bother me as much as the fact that he hadn't even told Ben all of this until last Christmas after it was all a done deal.

Apparently, Hal and Nicole, a California girl, had been quite the item long before he'd given her his mother's diamond ring before Christmas. But Ben didn't know anything until he met Nicole when he'd visited Hal for the holidays, and Hal had left Ben to tell me. The whole situation made me less than eager to meet Nicole or have much conversation with Hal, either.

"Not really but it looks like I'm going to anyway." While I wouldn't tell Ben the specifics of how I would likely meet his future stepmother, I'd definitely fill in Linnette. Maybe, I thought, the information would give her another smile today. I hoped it was good for a laugh for somebody.

* * *

Linnette wasn't all that thrilled when I told her about Nicole's second identity as Hal's fiancée. "If you want to back out on taking me to therapy, I'll understand."

I waved a hand, showing a lot more confidence than I really felt. "Not a problem. We were bound to run into each other somewhere anyway. And besides, I'm just the driver here. The therapy is for you, remember?"

"Right, but we usually look out for each other as Christian Friends. Why should this time be any different?"

If I had to list the ways Linnette had looked out for me so far, I'd run out of space long before I ran out of favors. She invited me to the group in the first place when she found me having a meltdown in the college bookstore where she's the assistant manager. She'd seen me through the death of my husband, and she'd helped me get the job at the Coffee Corner when I needed money and distraction. And all that was just in the first month she'd known me.

I owed her more already than I could say, and I told her so in a firm and friendly way. She wasn't thinking all that straight right now and I didn't want her to get feelings of guilt over something this minor. At least I could convince myself it would be minor. If I did things right perhaps I wouldn't ever run into Nicole.

I continued to convince myself of that in the evening when I stopped by the apartment quickly for a few things, planning to head back to Linnette's to spend the night. I had to give Ben a call back to explain why I'd asked about Nicole before, without telling him any more about Linnette. He knew her, and I figured that if she wanted to share her illness with him eventually she could do so.

For now all he needed to know was that my meeting Nicole had to do with "a Christian Friends thing" and that was enough explanation for him. My son viewed the activities of my all-female support group at church with as much enthusiasm as he did the Lifetime channel on cable.

I'd hung up talking to him and grabbed my books when the phone rang. At first I decided not to touch it, and then changed my mind when the Caller ID showed the Ventura County Sheriff's Department. "Hey, there. Staying late at work?" Only after I'd said that by way of greeting did I think that it might not be the handsome detective I expected on the other end of the line.

He laughed, obviously thinking the same thing. "If I were a little meaner I would have disguised my voice and tried to sell you tickets to a charity event," Ray said.

"Fortunately for me, you're not quite that mean. How are you doing, Detective Fernandez?"

"Well enough to wonder why you're being that formal, Gracie Lee."

"Hey, if you were offering to sell me charity tickets you might have me on speakerphone. Have to keep up appearances, don't I?"

"Nah, everybody that counts knows we're seeing each other, and they also know that you're no longer part of any case I'm involved in. The really trusted few even know that it isn't serious yet. Not that I wouldn't mind changing that."

My sigh was automatic. "Ray, I don't feel like going into that tonight." My reasons for not getting more involved with Ray all centered around faith, and the discussion got tangled every time we talked.

"You sound tired. What's up?"

I told him as much as Linnette and I agreed upon. There was a silence on his end of the line when I finished. "Wow. Now there's something that could get me praying for somebody else. You know how much I like Linnette. And I get the feeling that things might be even more serious than you're letting on."

Now I fell silent, leaving him to jump in again and fill the gap. "That's okay, don't confirm it. I would rather not know because legally I'd be skating on thin ice if I knew too much."

"What do you mean? Linnette said something

earlier I didn't understand and I forgot to ask her then."

Ray didn't disappoint me. If he ever gives up police work he can go straight to the college lecture scene. "California law, like most other states, has a pretty firm policy on some things, and talking about depression is one of them. If I heard from someone that they or someone they knew well had suicidal thoughts, or any ideas on taking action that might harm themselves, there is only one choice I can make. That person becomes an involuntary patient in a locked facility for at least seventy-two hours."

A chill ran down my spine. I thanked God that I hadn't said anything that might put Linnette in that situation. At least she knew about it in advance and had warned me. "I see. Thank you for explaining it to me."

"Any time. Now go keep your friend company and we'll talk in a day or two when we both have more time. If you've got a couple hours on the weekend, there are some movies out there we might both enjoy." I promised to think about it and we wished each other good night.

My relationship with Ray Fernandez was tenuous at best. He was a good man, honest and direct. Those qualities made him a more than competent detective. He looked the part, too, always handsome and sharply dressed. But he knew that after two marriages ending badly I wasn't about to get serious with somebody without a strong faith life. My sigh echoed through the front room of the apartment as I gathered my things to go back to Linnette's. We'd both need a little of that chocolate I packed tonight.

THREE

Wednesday I drove Linnette to her first appointment at Playa del Sol. Linnette acted as the navigator on a beautiful spring morning. It made both of us wish my car had a sunroof. Just the fact that she felt able to say that made me think things might be looking up for my friend.

With lattes in the cup holders, one of Ben's Christian rock CDs in the player and our sunglasses on, the mood felt as light as possible. The hospital was surrounded by two-story-tall palm trees and looked like a replica of the Spanish missions that dotted Southern California. Pale stucco and dark beams drew the eye away from the small windows and few doors. "Some of the units are lock-down," Linnette said softly as we parked. "That's why it looks so grim on the wings of the building. Where I'm going is open, though."

We went through a lobby area where both of us had our purses gone through by a security guard. Linnette got directed down a hallway while they ushered me into a small courtyard to wait. I carried my book bag, which passed inspection, and my pad of small sticky tabs to mark the places in the books that might prove to be good research for my thesis project. By the end of the summer my proposal would be due and I was getting nervous about it.

Several people walked back and forth through the courtyard while I read. I tried not to pay too much attention to anyone in case they wanted their privacy. At one point someone who looked like a hospital employee ushered another woman through toward where Linnette had gone. The woman she escorted drew my attention with her looks and gestures. Wiry and slightly askew in more ways than one, her clothing told me she lived at the hospital, at least temporarily. She wore sock-style slippers with vinyl-coated nonskid soles and a set of hospital gowns, one worn backward over the other to provide coverage.

"I used to be Diana, Princess of Wales, before they buried me," the woman said to no one in particular, doing a perfect imitation of the elegant wave made famous by the British royal family. Her dark brown hair made a halo around her head and she looked none too steady on her feet despite the traction of the slippers. The woman escorting her tried to keep her on track.

"Come on, Zoë, you need to get to therapy now. They don't like holding up the group for you, remember? And you promised Nicole that you'd work on timeliness this week," she chided. Her contrast to her patient couldn't have been more vivid. The woman in pale scrubs and sensible white clogs appeared to be a world away from the other one. Not only did she look professional and together, and at least ten years younger than her charge, she had at least six inches in height and about thirty pounds on her charge.

At first I wondered why they thought they needed someone that sturdy to escort a frail soul like Zoë. The nurse or aide, with a heavy braid of blond hair down her back, looked as though her ancestors brought some Viking stock to California. Meanwhile Zoë looked like a good puff of wind would blow her away. Then she did a turn and breakaway move that looked like something out of a kung fu movie. "There are agents at therapy. I can't go there without my protective gear," she said, sounding panicked.

The speed and force of her movement made me think about getting off my bench to head for the hills. I mean, I had no idea what her "agents" looked like and didn't want to be mistaken for one.

Something told me that wouldn't be healthy for either of us. Before I moved and scattered my books, the nurse had the situation defused.

Her response was quick for someone of her size, making me believe she'd had plenty of practice. In a heartbeat she had both of Zoë's shoulders in a firm grasp, turning her toward their destination again. "We've talked about that, Zoë, remember? The protection is built into the walls here, and it's not safe to have you carrying around your foil and insulation. Now let's get to your group before Nicole gets annoyed."

Distracted, Zoë gave the royal wave again. "Nicole never gets annoyed with me. She's part of my adoring public." After that they cruised out of sight with no more incidents. It took me a few minutes to settle back down to my reading. Linnette, I figured, might have some stories to share when she got back.

I'd almost gotten back into my work when I felt a presence in front of me. Looking up I saw the employee who had been escorting Zoë. "First time here?" she asked, smiling.

She looked perceptive and sympathetic at the same time. I noticed that her ID badge said Catalina and listed her as an RN. "It is. Do I look that much like a deer in the headlights?"

She laughed softly. "Not all that much, but out

of the corner of my eye I could see your reaction to the patient I was escorting. I wanted to stop to reassure you that almost everybody here is basically harmless. They have their own demons haunting them, but outside civilians don't usually have any problems with the patients."

"Thanks. It's nice to know that. My name's Gracie Lee and you might see me here a few more times. I'm a friend's designated driver for some therapy sessions."

"Great. I'm Cat and normally I'm on the day shift with ambulatory inpatients, so we'll probably run into each other if you keep driving your friend. Hang in there, and thanks for doing something kind for somebody else. You'd be amazed how many people get abandoned by their friends once mental illness enters their life."

I waved a hand automatically. "That won't happen with my friend. She's probably got half a dozen folks who will stand by her. It's nice meeting you, Cat. See you soon."

She nodded and headed toward the door to what I assumed was inpatient services at a brisk clip. It made me feel good that the people here had caring, competent people looking after them. Even if Cat was the cream of the crop, at least there were some like her working in what had to be a difficult situation. Once I started working on citations in the thickest of my reference books I lost track of things around me again.

Soon I felt rather than saw a smaller person than Cat standing next to me and before I looked in that direction I opened my mouth to apologize to Linnette for keeping her waiting. The words died as I looked up into hazel doe eyes much too young, in my estimation, to be my ex-husband's next wife. However the name tag on her white coat said Nicole Barnes, so that's who she had to be. Behind the woman's white-coated figure Linnette looked uncomfortable as she shrugged silently. Her gesture clearly said she'd tried her best to avoid this.

Putting down my book I stood to be on equal ground. "Hi, Nicole. I'm Gracie Lee. But you seem to know that already." Might as well be up front with everything. Whatever relationship I was going to have with this young woman could be as cordial as possible. It wouldn't hurt me any, and could make life easier for Ben.

"Hi. I recognized you from Ben's graduation pictures. Ms. Parks didn't tell me you were her friend, honest." Nicole Barnes sounded even younger than she looked, her apology made more tentative by the upward questioning lilt at the end of each sentence.

Standing up, the only satisfaction I had in facing

her was that even in flats I was taller. Of course I also outweighed her by more than I felt like calculating but I didn't want to dwell on that thought just yet.

The oversize lab coat and badge clipped to the collar spoke of authority but Nicole didn't look comfortable with it. A classic silk tee in muted green and jeans in a single-digit size didn't quite meet at a level slightly higher than the crest of her tiny hipbones. At least she didn't seem to be sporting a belly-button piercing.

"I wouldn't have minded if Linnette had said something. We were bound to meet somewhere soon anyway, Nicole." I put my hand out and she grasped it quickly with dry, cool fingers, letting go just as speedily. I said silent thanks that she wasn't the type to give me an air kiss or sorority sister hug. Handling either one would be too much today.

She gave a wry smile that almost made her look like a woman of thirty. "I keep looking around when we get coffee someplace or go to a restaurant, thinking we might run into you. I haven't gone anyplace in sweats or without wearing makeup since we moved to California."

I couldn't imagine that I'd intimidate anybody this young and attractive just by living in the same county, but I didn't say anything. If we stood here making small talk too long I'd lapse into something catty like asking her how the wedding plans were going, and if Hal's mother had tried to horn in on planning this ceremony, too.

Before the silence got awkward Nicole got an odd look on her face and started fishing in her lab coat pocket. "Cell phone on vibrate," she said by way of explanation, looking at the miniscule screen. "Excuse me. *What?* No, Paige, this really isn't a good time," she said into the phone, smiling apologetically.

I murmured something about actually having coffee together sometime soon, she nodded while listening and mercifully soon Linnette and I found ourselves in the car ready to leave.

"Well, we got out of there in record time, didn't we? I'm sorry if you wanted to hang around," I told her. "I was so focused on escaping without saying anything I'd regret later that I didn't give you much attention."

She waved a hand in dismissal. "Don't worry about it. There's only so much of a group situation like that I can take right now. I'm still feeling wiped out after about an hour of concentration." She'd likened the beginning of recovery state she was in to getting over a bad case of the flu, and right now I could see what she meant.

We picked up lunch at a nearby chain restaurant in Camarillo. I made a mental note to start clipping coupons out of the paper for places on our route.

"So how did your first session go? I realize you can't say much," I said quickly, not wanting any details of anything I shouldn't be privy to.

"It was interesting."

"Hmm. When Ben was little that phrase was what I taught him to say when he tried something new at somebody else's table and ate a bite or two even if he didn't like it." Of course maybe Linnette had a totally different meaning.

Her answering smile said I was on target. "Same here. Tom's mother fixed a number of 'interesting' casseroles for Steph and Karin over the years. And that's pretty much what group therapy felt like. A few things I wasn't used to, served up in a way that made me only slightly uncomfortable."

"I think I saw one of your group come through the courtyard." I gave a thumbnail sketch of Zoë and her behavior.

"She was mostly silent during group. I'd have to guess she has some form of schizophrenia and perhaps been without medication for a while. It was clear from things Nicole asked that Zoë was homeless or close to it before she came to the hospital this time."

"How could she possibly have a chance of staying on medication if she didn't have a place to call her own?"

I could see Linnette shaking her head. "It's part

of a cycle for some people. If they feel all right on meds, eventually they stop taking them because they convince themselves they don't need them. Then everything falls apart slowly. The thing that seemed to surprise us all the most was when Zoë announced she would be leaving the hospital next week."

"Whoa. The woman I saw didn't look like somebody who could function on her own yet. And from what you've said, she doesn't have much support."

"Next to none. Nicole looked disturbed too but then she checked something on a clipboard and saw that Zoë was right." Linnette shook her head. "If I felt a little more stable and a lot more trusting in life right now I might have offered to take her in for a while." She looked down at her mostly-empty soup bowl. "I can still trust in God, but trusting in the system that would let somebody like Zoë out of the hospital is something else again."

"She's a ways past the kind of hurting we can help with Christian Friends, isn't she?"

"I'm afraid so." Linnette looked down at the table. "Right now I feel a ways past it myself. I'm going to need to hand over the reins for a while, Gracie Lee. Do you think that with some coaching you could take over for me?"

Wow. That came out of nowhere. I felt very thankful that I hadn't just taken a sip of the iced tea lifted to my lips. "Me? Isn't anybody else trained to do that? Dot or somebody?" Virtually everyone in our Christian Friends group had been there longer than I had.

"Not really. Besides, you have the gift for it. I can see it."

"If you say so. Isn't there real training for this somehow?"

"There is, but in a situation like this I can show you the ropes. And Pastor George will be there to lean on. You don't have to agree to anything right now over a bowl of soup."

"Good. Because I don't think I could." Agreeing to lead our group any time wasn't something I'd be likely to do for anybody else. For Linnette I'd at least consider it.

Maybe I should thank her, I thought. Suddenly I'd lost all desire for the dessert I'd been considering. Her invitation would save me at least five hundred calories.

After two group therapy sessions and a week of rest, Linnette felt ready to go back to work. "I can't afford much more time away. Besides, there's enough work stacking up that if I don't go back soon I'll be afraid to go back at all."

This week I still served as chauffeur, so we had our conversation while heading to Playa del Sol for one more round, then a couple hours' work for both of us on campus. Huge blossoming purple trees ringing the hospital parking lot announced the season.

"Wow. The jacarandas are all blooming. They weren't last week, were they?" Linnette looked so vulnerable it made me hide a quick flash of tears.

"No, they really weren't. I think you would have noticed."

She shrugged. "You've got more confidence than I do in my ability to recover quickly, then. For me, today's one of the first days I feel like a functioning human being. I might not have noticed an entire circus parade before this."

I'd worked my way through two thick research books and a stack of journal articles during my stays in the courtyard waiting for Linnette during therapy. Today I'd just settled down to make more notations when the door from the reception area burst open.

"We have to work things out better from now on," Nicole said sharply. Papers and folders poked out of a canvas tote slung over one shoulder, her hair needed attention and I suspected that the scuffed flats she wore weren't her first choice for work.

Behind her trailed Zoë, who was dressed in a colorful assortment of street clothes that had the air of being gleaned from a thrift store sale rack.

Her hair looked as neat as Nicole's today and she had the demeanor of a sullen teenager to match her outfit. As they crossed the courtyard Nicole lost a piece of paper from her bag. When she bent to pick it up she saw me.

Before I could say anything she glared at me, stuffed the paper back hastily and moved on. I kept from saying anything nasty, just barely. Later when I reflected on the scene I wished I'd said some little thing to make an awkward situation more pleasant. If I'd had any idea that would be the last time I'd see Nicole, I would have been nicer. The entire scene was over before I could consider what it really meant.

Apparently, Zoë was out of the hospital, and perhaps Nicole had even given her a ride to the therapy session from wherever she was staying. I forgot to say anything about it all to Linnette while I drove her to work. As it turned out, that was our last opportunity for a lengthy conversation for two days.

The rest of the week dumped finals and final projects on me, and Linnette was catching up at work while still only putting in five hours a day. Thursday afternoon Ben, finished with finals and out of the dorm until next year, came into the apartment with almost all of his possessions, enough to fill his old car twice. After the second trip he spent about an hour putting everything in his room and clearing a path in and out, promptly vanishing to go see his steady girlfriend Cai Li.

Friday, Ben mostly lounged in the apartment while I finished up my semester on campus. When I got home late in the afternoon he was heading out again, another evening with Cai Li. Linnette and I split a delivery pizza and a romantic comedy on DVD that evening, both too tired to make a lot of conversation. Still, it was a happier kind of tired than we'd shared in a while. I went home early and went straight to bed.

In the morning it didn't surprise me to be able to shower, dress and be ready to face the day without hearing anything from Ben. Early morning on a Saturday, especially his first one of the summer, wasn't a time I'd expect to see him up. What did surprise me was his open bedroom door and neatly made empty bed. Casting about in my mind, I realized I hadn't heard anything all night that sounded like him coming home. I don't worry when he's at school but my "mom radar" kicks in the moment he's home.

Calling his cell phone only got his message. In ten minutes I had overcome my reservations and called Hal. He answered before the second ring. "Nicole?"

"No, Gracie Lee. And we've got trouble. Ben didn't come home last night."

"Gracie, he's almost nineteen, healthy and male. Besides, I don't have time for this right now."

My panic flamed into anger. "You don't have time for your own son?"

"Not now. I've got bigger problems and I need to keep this phone line free. So either come over here or deal with Ben yourself."

I had a dial tone in my ear before I could remind my prickly ex-husband I didn't know exactly where "here" was, having never been to his new Ventura County home. It galled me to have to get out my Thomas guide and look up how to find his street. Since it was for Ben, I did it, grumbling all the while.

Leaving a note for Ben in case he showed up at the apartment, I grabbed my best map and headed to the car. Whatever had Hal this upset meant I'd have to go to him if we were going to decide together what to do about Ben. I had no idea that in an hour I'd be back on the road home, knowing little more than I had before and still waiting for another phone to ring.

FOUR

Finding Hal's house wasn't as difficult as I thought it would be. Fortunately, I had looked in Ben's room before I left home to see if he had the gate code written down. When I reached Hal's gated community, no little guardhouse decorated the gate, which seemed like lax security to me. That wasn't my concern, though, so I just punched the code in at the gate and breezed through.

Tuscany Hills—the somewhat pretentious name of the development—could have been called "McMansions R Us." Maybe eight feet of space divided each two-story brick pile from the next in most cases. The cul-de-sac with Hal's house had slightly larger lots. His driveway wound around behind the house to a turnaround courtyard flanked by a large patio, a three-bay garage that could have housed a family of four, and what looked like a small guest cottage or a large pool house.

We stood and had our argument with each other in the middle of this large piece of concrete, trendily textured to look like cobblestone, until I got tired of the whole thing. "Look, you're too worried about Nicole to think about anything else. I can see that." I pulled a piece of paper out of my purse and wrote on it. "Here's my cell phone number, since I don't imagine you have it. Call me if you hear from Ben, or when Nicole comes home."

Hal looked relieved. I imagine so, because there would be one less woman on his case, at least for a few hours. "When do the in-laws come in?"

"That's the problem, Gracie Lee. I'm not really sure. Nicole and her mom and sister talk to each other a lot by phone, but she hasn't kept me up with all the details. All I know is that they'll be here sometime in the afternoon and the guesthouse needs to be ready."

I gave him a quick hug because we both needed one. "Hang in there. Hopefully we'll all laugh about this in a week or two." He didn't argue with me, a bad sign. When Hal wasn't contentious with me he had to be really preoccupied. All the way down his long, curved driveway I could see his expression in my rearview mirror. He looked way too much like a lost child for me to be angry with him. I said silent prayers for all of us, Hal and Nicole and Ben and me, while I drove home.

Once back at the apartment I used my excess energy to scrub the bathroom and clean closets, both phones near me all the time. Morning turned into early afternoon and still neither phone rang. I used the apartment phone once briefly to call Linnette to let her know what was happening.

Half an hour later she appeared at my door bearing a warm loaf of bread and lots of sympathy. "You caught me at just the right time. The bread machine was beeping when the phone rang." Her hug felt a lot better than Hal's had earlier. With Linnette I had no odd feelings about hugging her back and taking comfort from her. Linnette was a friend in a way Hal had never been, even when we were married.

"So it looks like you're coming around a little," I told her, impressed by the loaf of bread and her general demeanor. Hair combed, with clean and neat jeans and T-shirt on, she'd even put on makeup on a Saturday.

She lifted one shoulder in a shrug. "I'm trying. At least I'm feeling a lot more comfortable being alone, and it didn't take me more than two hours to get up, dressed and put the bread in the machine. It's progress."

I couldn't agree with her more, and I thanked God for that progress today. "How long do you think I should wait before calling Ray? I know that for adults they usually have you wait twenty-four hours to report someone missing."

"When was the last time you saw Ben? It has to be going on at least eighteen hours, doesn't it?"

I thought for a minute. "Yes, but I'm not sure if the first five or six hours count because I knew where he was then, or at least I think that he was with Cai Li because that's where he said he'd be."

"Have you called his girlfriend's parents? Or the girl's cell phone?"

"No and no. Both are good ideas, though. I've been so focused on Ben, I wasn't thinking straight. But I've got her parents' number someplace, just not her cell." There had never been a reason so far for me to call her cell. I hadn't even met her family yet and now I had to call them and possibly turn their lives upside down, if they hadn't been ruined already.

I realized, though, her parents or someone from the police or fire department would already have called me if something dire had happened to both of them. Okay, so it wasn't the greatest of relief, but a bit of comfort anyway.

After a few minutes I found Cai Li's parents' home phone number and called, Linnette sitting next to me holding her breath just a little. The phone rang enough times that I waited for a machine to pick up. Instead a slightly breathless voice said, "Hello?"

It sounded familiar. "Cai Li?"

"Yes. Mrs. Harris?" With someone her age I didn't want to quibble about whether I preferred Mrs. or Ms. especially when I felt so surprised to have her answer the phone.

"It sure is. Would you happen to know where Ben is?"

The silence on the other end made me want to shake the phone or shriek. Finally she said "Didn't he get home yet? He left here maybe an hour ago."

I kept my questions to myself, including where the two of them had been all night and what they had been doing. Those could both be answered by Ben once he showed up or I found him. I really hoped he showed up soon because if I had to go find him things could get grim in a hurry. For now I thanked Cai Li for telling me about Ben, said goodbye and hung up. By the time I finished telling Linnette about my conversation we could hear a car pulling up on the driveway below the apartment. "Do you want me to leave?" Linnette stood looking at the door.

"Not yet. If you stay awhile maybe I won't yell as much." Worth a try, anyway.

Sounds from outside indicated that someone with large feet climbed the stairs, then the door-knob rattled and Ben stepped into the room. "Hi, Mom. Hi, Mrs. Parks. I hope I didn't worry you too much. We totally lost track of time."

"You must have. Is there anything else you'd like to tell me?" Ben smiled a bit dreamily.

"Yeah, I guess there is. I think I'm engaged."

Linnette excused herself quickly before the yelling began. She left just in time. Actually what followed wasn't as much yelling as it was very one-sided discussion in a louder tone of voice. Ben shut down when I started firing questions at him, preferring to give me one- or two-word answers.

None of them informed me much. It took an hour's worth of long questions and short answers for me to get anywhere. "So let me see if I've got this straight." I tried to relax my jaw so my words didn't come out from between clenched teeth. "You and Cai Li sat up all night, first in the park then in her living room and then at a diner where you had breakfast and the two of you decided to get married?"

His bright blue eyes, blazing with defiance, reminded me why similar looks from his father helped lead to a divorce all those years ago. "You make it sound dumb when you put it that way. We're in love, Mom. We both know we want to be together."

"Forever? I mean, I haven't shown you the best track record, Ben, but you have to go into something as serious as marriage knowing that this is the person you want to spend the rest of your life with. It's not a decision I'd recommend anybody make at nineteen or twenty." I knew Cai Li was a little older than Ben, and I gave him the benefit of his next birthday, coming up in a few weeks.

"You did. Dad did. And your parents let you."

"Not happily, they didn't. And they were right. We didn't have the maturity we needed to stick together when things got really rough." I understood now why Ray and guys in general ran their hands through their hair in frustration as if they wanted to pull it out. Talking to the stucco wall out back would have given me more results.

"We're different. We know what we're doing. And besides, we've got God on our side."

Okay, now that I couldn't argue with. Maybe things would have turned out a whole bunch differently if Hal and I had been more religious back then. Maybe if he'd read the Bible more Hal would have really gotten that part where it says that a man should leave his mother and become one with his wife. Right, as if that would have magically solved all our problems.

I felt as though I'd run out of steam. "We'll discuss this more at length today, I promise you. But I told your dad we'd call him when you showed up. How about doing that while I get us something cold to drink?"

Ben looked nonplussed. It felt good to surprise him, even though his surprise right now didn't hold a candle to what he'd sprung on me. "Fine. I'll do that."

He stepped across the room to the corner, not as much to avoid me as to get into the spot where our cell phones had the best reception. While he did that I went over to the kitchen and got two glasses, ice and some lemonade out of the refrigerator. That way I could work off some of my excess energy and I wouldn't be tempted to eavesdrop on his conversation with Hal.

He was just closing his cell phone when I brought in our glasses of cold lemonade. "I think we're going to want to put this in travel mugs."

"Oh? What's going on?"

"Dad says Nicole still hasn't shown up but her mom and sister have. And he wants me to go over there to talk. I'm not sure if he wants to yell at me or if he just wants somebody on his side with the in-laws there."

"Okay, that explains why your lemonade is going in a travel mug. How about me?"

Ben had a sheepish grin. "You have to explain to me what's going on with Nicole in the first place. It didn't sound like a good thing to ask Dad right now. Besides, I've been up for about thirty-two hours. You don't really want me to drive over there, do you?"

I didn't. So the lemonade went into mugs with

lids, and I explained as much as I knew about Hal and Nicole's situation until Ben fell asleep in the front seat, looking more like a boy than a man who was contemplating marriage.

This time we went inside the two-story front entryway of Hal's mansionette. I stilled any desire to make comments about the decorating style, where a spare modern palette in white, red and black reigned in the living room on one side of the hall. Warring with that, the dining room held what I knew were the Harris family treasures in cherrywood with damask seat cushions; a set of furniture I'd never expected to see anywhere but Tennessee.

Obviously, Nicole rated higher with Lillian Harris than I ever had to get the heirlooms. I wondered what would happen if Hal's mother caught wind of this last-minute disappearance of her soon-to-be daughter-in-law. If I got a minute I'd ask Hal when his mother planned to make her appearance. Or his father, for that matter. They'd been divorced for a number of years and I didn't always keep track of them the way I should have.

He looked as if he would welcome his mother right now. "So you think you're engaged?" he snapped at Ben the moment we cleared the threshold. "Don't you think I've got enough on my mind right now without this kind of nonsense?"

Standing together Hal and Ben looked to be the same height, somewhere a bit over six feet. Ben, of course, had the lanky frame of youth but with the promise of the solidity his father already showed. My son's face still sported spots of color high in his cheeks from sleeping in the car, and further fueled by Hal's remark.

I wanted to rush in between them before anything was said they'd regret later, but at the same time I knew that I couldn't help either side of this argument. Still, it hurt to watch. "Did you ever stop to think that this wasn't about you, Dad? That maybe it was about me, and Cai and what we want together?"

"You're not old enough to know what you want. Neither of you is. What brought this on, anyway? She's not…"

"Hal, don't go there." I couldn't let him finish that thought. "You're upset about Nicole and this surprise on top of it. But take a minute to think straight, okay?"

He sighed. "Right, Gracie Lee. I forgot that all of you are such serious churchgoers that stuff like a shotgun wedding isn't possible. Certainly not with *your* son involved, anyway." He spit the word with more ferocity than I expected and for a moment I could feel pain there, the pain of a man who knew he wasn't the biggest influence in his son's life.

More than fifteen years of raising Ben on my own with only occasional input from his father should have prepared me for this moment but it didn't. "Hey, reach back that far and at least remember what prompted us to get married, Hal. You know as well as I do that it wasn't an unplanned pregnancy, so that shouldn't be your first thought with Ben and Cai Li, either."

"No, the unplanned pregnancy part came later. When we got married it was just because we were young and stupid. Which is what I'm trying to point out to you." He turned to face Ben. "Do you want to blow your whole future, both of you? She can't be worth it."

It was all I could do not to yell at him. I mean, he'd managed to hurt everybody else in the room in one shot. And his words obviously didn't convince Ben of anything except that his father knew nothing. Ben looked at me and I could see the anger rising in him. I was praying silently, fervently now for the wisdom to do and say the right things here. The pain between us felt like a living thing.

I took a deep breath and let it out slowly. "You know, I'm really afraid that we'll all say things here that we'll regret in a big way if we keep this discussion going. Maybe some of us already have said more than is needed. One thing that we can all agree on is that your dad and I both want what's best for you, and we love you, Ben. It may be difficult for you to see that right now because we aren't expressing ourselves very well."

"You can say that again," Ben said, almost under his breath. At any rate, I'd managed to defuse the situation a little. He still looked like an angry young man, but with a bit more control now.

Hal stood silently, looking at the two of us. "I hate to say so, Gracie Lee, but you're right for a change. Ben, I'm just so uptight right now with everything else happening that if we keep talking about this I will say it all wrong."

Ben's expression clearly said he didn't think his father would say the right thing even without being under pressure, but at least he didn't voice it. "So if we don't talk about this anymore do you want Mom and me to go home?"

"Not right away. Back there in the guesthouse my future mother-in-law and Nicole's sister Paige are ready to eat me alive. I could use some backup."

I hadn't met Nicole's family but I could guess why they were angry. "Are they blaming you for Nicole's disappearance?"

Hal exhaled noisily. "Of course. Perfect little Nicole wouldn't have done this without provocation from her horrible old fiancé. And they certainly are rubbing in the 'old' part."

Ben shook his head. "Dad, what do you expect?

I met her sister Paige once, remember? She's way closer to me in age than to you. And she makes Nicole look like a rocket scientist."

I shot Ben a glance to tell him not to malign Nicole. He nodded almost imperceptibly. "Sorry, Dad. That wasn't a nice way to put that. I mean, Nicole is plenty bright. But her sister isn't going to be looking for deep reasons for Nicole's not showing up."

Hal sighed. "I hate to say it, but you're right there. That's why I'm asking you to stick around awhile. You two at least won't blame me because Nicole isn't home. Will you?" He had a sad-eyed-puppy look that had won him a lot of arguments when we were married. By now I'm immune.

"That depends. Is there anything you haven't told us yet about last night? You two didn't get into an argument or anything, did you?" Hal had matured some in the last fifteen years, but he still tended to snap more quickly than he should. Given a sensitive young woman like Nicole, whose job led her to read meaning into everything he said to her whether it existed or not, that could mean trouble.

"No arguments. At least not over anything big. I mean, we're two weeks from a wedding that her mother is determined to make the production of the century. There's bound to be arguments over stuff like that."

"True. I can still remember what we went through with your mother and mine even over a small wedding last time. So how do you think Ben and I will help defuse things?"

Hal sighed again. "Maybe you won't. But at least come out there with me so that I can introduce you. If I'm lucky they won't take any more potshots at me with company present."

I wasn't so sure he was right there, but I went with him anyway, Ben following behind us. We only made it halfway across the pavement toward the guesthouse when the door flew open and a woman charged out. Her progress was only partially checked by noticing Hal wasn't alone. She stopped a few feet from the door, glaring at him.

If I hadn't been out here in Southern California for a few years I might have thought this woman wasn't very upset by her daughter's disappearance. Her expensive knit pantsuit showed more disturbance than her face. But out here everybody over forty has had some "work done" it seems, and botox injections are as common as bottled water. And if I did the math right, Nicole's mother had to be in her early fifties.

"Tell me you've heard from Nicole and that's why you're out here," she said frostily.

"Sorry, Ellie, but I haven't heard any more than you have. I just wanted Ben and his mother to meet you before they went home." Hal tried to look as placating as possible. I knew what a task that was for him.

A second woman appeared at the doorway to the guesthouse. While Nicole didn't look much like her mother except in slenderness and stature, this woman who I assumed had to be Paige was definitely her mother's daughter. Paige's hair color looked more realistic in ash-blond, and her face was still naturally unlined. "Is she home? I heard noise out here." When she saw us her look was a scornful duplicate of her mother's expression. While Ellie glared at Hal, Paige was looking past him to the two of us.

"Oh. You." Maybe this wasn't anybody's finest moment here, but Paige's disdain for Ben made me want to shriek at her. That would have solved nothing, so I just let her mother quell any further remarks with another glare. This caused Paige to toss her two-hundred-dollar haircut around and huff out air, flaring her nostrils like a thoroughbred filly. "Well, I thought it was maybe *family*."

Before anyone could say anything else the sound of a phone ringing filled the air. Hal reached into his pocket and answered it. The lowering of his shoulders told me immediately it wasn't Nicole on the other end of the conversation. "Yes, it is. I called because Nicole hasn't been here today. Do you know where she is?"

He listened a moment, shoulders slumping even lower. "Yes, her car is here. She didn't say anything…strange that you remember?"

No one else said anything, all listening to his end of the conversation and filling in the blanks for ourselves. It was over soon enough anyway and Hal closed his phone and put it away. "That was Cat from the hospital where Nicole works. She was one of the two women that went out with Nicole last night. She says she hasn't seen Nicole since about one when they all went their separate ways."

I realized with a start that I'd met the person Hal was talking to. She was the nurse from the courtyard, the first day I'd taken Linnette for her therapy session. Before I could say anything, Ellie jumped in.

"Cat. Would that be Catalina?" How anybody that much shorter than Hal could look down her nose at him as effectively as Ellie Barnes did was beyond me. "I wish you'd said something while you were still speaking with her. I've got things to say to that young woman. She never showed up for her last bridesmaid's dress fitting."

Okay, that did me in. Her daughter is missing and the most Ellie Barnes can say is one of the bridesmaids is remiss in her fitting appointments? Nicole's mother didn't seem to think much of me anyway, so I had nothing to lose. I resolved to tell her right now what I thought of her. I wasn't on the guest list for the wedding anyway, so she couldn't uninvite me.

Hal could still sense my thoughts enough to know what I'd say next and for once I felt relieved when he broke in before I could say anything else. "I think it's time Ben and his mom went home. We can do formal introductions once Nicole is back, Ellie." He turned his back on his future mother-in-law before Ellie could tell him how rude he appeared. He must have shot Ben a look to communicate something over my head as he grabbed my elbow, quite gently given the circumstances, and ushered me away. I'd never been walked to my car as quickly as it happened now. I didn't even get a chance to tell him "thank you" for keeping me out of more trouble.

Ben and I were on the outside of the subdivision before we spoke again. "Wow. I think Dad's seriously outclassed there. I hope Nicole shows up soon. Otherwise Dad and her mom are going to get into it a whole lot worse than we were going to back there."

I couldn't agree with him more. If Nicole Barnes still wanted to get married with everyone on speaking terms, she better not let the sun go down before she got back home.

FIVE

Ben and I stayed in the apartment together on Saturday night, but there wasn't much talking. There was plenty of glaring and some short starts at conversations that didn't go much of anyplace. He napped some and spent a good deal of time on his cell phone with Cai Li, or on his computer in the bedroom with the door open, all the sounds from the machine indicating that he was doing a fair amount of instant messaging.

He agreed to get up and go to church with me on Sunday morning as long as I would go to the service where Cai Li played in the praise band. I didn't see any problem with that, and when Pastor George's sermon topic was "Forgiveness" I imagine each of us was thinking the same thing…that the other person probably needed forgiveness more. It took me a few minutes afterward to feel bad about my thoughts and to do a little fence-mending with Ben once the service ended. He still answered pretty brusquely but we managed a brief hug and a bit of a smile at each other. Then he went up front to talk to Cai Li and I headed to the fellowship between services to hang with my friends and find some sympathy.

"If we didn't already have a meeting scheduled for Wednesday I would call one just for you," Linnette said, coming up to give me another hug. "Maybe instead of going to any of the adult Bible study classes this morning, a few of us need to have our own private meeting instead."

"I wouldn't argue with that. Dot should be here anytime and I'll look for Heather if you'll look for Lexy."

Linnette nodded. "I'll try to round up Paula if I can and maybe even snag us a private pot of coffee." Now I knew she was on the road to recovery. Linnette was back to being the social director of our little group of friends. Here was one facet of my life that showed some improvement this morning.

Fifteen minutes later the Christian Friends, at least our small group of Wednesday night regulars, gathered around a table in the fellowship hall. As good as her word, Linnette poured coffee into everyone's cup while Dot passed the plate of cookies she brought to the table.

"Nobody thinks best on an empty stomach and

I bet you haven't eaten much of anything in the last day or so." Leave it to my landlady to get to the heart of the matter.

"You're right. Between Ben being gone most of yesterday and his announcement once he got home, I haven't paid much attention to food." Dot waved the plate of oatmeal-raisin cookies under my nose and I took several. She knew enough about me to pick my favorite, and these looked home-baked, loaded with plump, golden raisins.

"So fill in the rest of us on what happened with the two of you so far. Linnette certainly didn't tell us anything," Paula said, stirring her coffee. She's a slight Asian woman whose job as a Realtor means she's usually dressed to the nines and on her cell phone closing a deal. Paula and I didn't always see eye-to-eye with each other but today she looked genuinely concerned.

I fortified myself with the rest of a cookie and a few sips of my coffee, then told the group what had been going on since Friday night. Lexy stayed silent until I got to the part about Nicole still being missing last night. "So in the middle of everything with Ben you drove him over to Hal's place and back?"

"Going to Hal's place was the only way to have Ben's father participate in the discussion. And this was one of those situations where we needed to be together."

"And did he say what you expected him to say?" I didn't know quite where Lexy was going with this but there was no point in not answering. Besides, my friend the entertainment lawyer always wore one of those expressions that made me want to answer her questions. How anybody could combine the looks of blond cheerleader and a legal shark like Alexis Adams did was beyond me. She pulled it off, though. Someday I want to see her in a courtroom.

"He said about what I should have expected. That doesn't mean it was what I wanted him to say. He tried to talk Ben out of this engagement but for all the wrong reasons."

"Then what are the right reasons?" Heather asked quietly. Of everyone there I would have expected her to back me up the most. As a single mom following a disastrous engagement to my late husband, I thought she would be on my side. Especially since she taught people Ben and Cai Li's age at the local community college. Today she let me down. "And couldn't there be as many right reasons why Ben and his girlfriend should be engaged?"

"But they're so young. And there are so many other things they should be doing instead." I tried not to sound too strident. It gave me a start to realize how much I sounded like my mother had twenty years ago when she'd tried to argue me out of marrying Hal.

"Let me ask you a question, and take a moment to think about the answer first. Are all those things you think they should be doing things they couldn't do while engaged to each other?" Dot tilted her head, ready to listen just like everyone's favorite silver-haired aunt. With her sparkling eyes questioning me over the half-glasses she wore for reading, I felt as though my books were overdue at the library.

I did as she'd asked and thought about things. My heart sank as I considered my answer. "Not all of them. I want Ben to finish school, and for that matter I'd want anybody he married to finish school if that was what she intended to do. These days there aren't many worthwhile jobs that don't need a college degree."

"Or more." Lexy piped up, reminding us all of her extra three years to get that law degree. "Steve and I waited until after we finished law school to get married, but I don't know if that was the best idea." Her expression told me she was reminded of their problems having a baby—problems that probably weren't helped by waiting until their late twenties to marry and even later to start a family. After four years of trying to have a baby, Lexy still yearned for a child.

"Okay, maybe some of you have a point. There are still so many questions I want to ask somebody.

I want to make sure they really think this through. And they're both scholarship students."

Paula made a sour face. "Well, I'd hope a Christian school that preached purity outside marriage would welcome their scholarship students marrying. It wouldn't make much sense otherwise. If they have penalties for getting married while in school, they don't know young people very well."

She had a point. This whole conversation had been nearly the reverse of what I'd expected. Paula appeared to be on the same wavelength I was on, Lexy and Heather seemed to be arguing for early marriage, and Linnette limited her activity to pouring coffee. At least nobody voiced speculations about the kids' reasons for marriage as Hal had started to. But then, everyone here knew both of them; many of the group saw Cai Li lead the contemporary praise band every Sunday.

We sat in silence for a little while, several people concentrating on cookies. Paula set down her coffee cup. "Okay then, if that's anywhere near settled, I want to hear about the runaway bride," she piped up. Now *this* sounded more like the Paula I knew and loved as a sister in Christ even when she drove me crazy. I didn't have to like Paula Choi all the time, but I did have to try and love her. Someday perhaps I will understand the mystery of God's sense of humor on instructions like that one, but today isn't the day.

Why are so many people out there that are prickly so difficult to love? And why did those folks seem to show up in my life in bunches? Maybe there would be a phone message on my machine when we got home from church that would alleviate one difficult bunch of people from my life. I really hoped that Nicole had made her way home overnight. It still might be an uncomfortable sort of wedding after the bride going AWOL for a little while, but at least I'd have a lot less contact with Hal and his family in the next two weeks.

Despite my wishes, I got home and the machine just wasn't blinking. Hope springs eternal, though, and by noon I'd convinced myself that Hal must be so busy now that Nicole returned that he had no time to call.

Of course when I called, that didn't seem to be the case. Hal still sounded panicky and stressed as he told me Nicole was still missing. "Did you sleep at all?" I asked him.

"A little. On the sofa." The mental picture I formed of my lanky ex-husband on the sofa I'd seen yesterday made me think that he must be awfully sore by now.

"Have you filed a missing person's report?"

There was silence for a while. "Not yet. Ellie thinks it's a bad idea."

"Why would that be a bad idea? Doesn't she want to find Nicole as quickly as possible?"

Hal sighed. "I'm beginning to wonder. She's more worried about the embarrassment if the report became public than looking for Nicole right away. Besides, I'm not sure how to do this."

The implication appeared to be that I did know how to file a missing person's report. I held my breath, trying to convince myself that I should just be quiet and let Hal come right out and ask for what he wanted instead of hinting. Still, I had an idea how to file the report, having intended to file one when my former mother-in-law, Edna Peete, went missing after her son's murder. That time I'd stepped back and let her blood relatives do the filing instead, which turned out to be a bad idea. If I'd pushed ahead and reported her missing right away, things might have turned out differently.

Remembering that mistake made me change my mind about helping Hal. "Let me hang up and make a few calls. In about twenty minutes I can probably tell you what to do."

"Thanks, Gracie Lee. I owe you one." The relief in his voice was palpable. Temptation to tell him to work off his debt by talking to his son at length rose instantly but I pushed it away. No matter what went on with Nicole and Hal, Ben and I would more than likely be the ones to work out our own problems. His father's tendency to avoid serious issues had been a problem when we divorced, and nothing had changed on that front.

Before I could voice any of these thoughts Hal had hung up. Calling Ray would be more pleasant than listening to Hal anyway.

Surprisingly, Ray picked up his cell phone after only two rings. "Hey, there. Tell me you missed me so much you just had to call to say hello."

I sighed. "Hi, Ray. I do miss you. And I do want to say hello."

"Aha. But I bet there's more."

"You are getting to know me way too well, mister."

He laughed. "Not nearly well enough for my tastes. But I won't start that argument now. What's on your mind, Gracie?"

"How do I file a missing person's report? No, wait, before you worry, let me rephrase that. How does somebody file a missing person's report?"

"Good. I'm glad it's not Ben you're asking about. Tell me it's not something to do with Linnette."

That made me smile. It felt good that Ray showed that much concern for a mutual friend. "You can breathe easy. Linnette's fine and Ben's been home about twenty-four hours. Now, he thinks he's engaged, but that's a story for when we get together."

"Aw, you can't spring that on me and not expect me to want to see you now. Coffee at Starbucks?"

"Sure. Which one of the seven locations between your house and mine should we choose?" He picked one, told me to give him half an hour and I hung up to get ready myself. Seeing Ray required a bit better attire than the shorts I'd changed into after church.

While still getting ready I realized I hadn't gotten a firm answer on how to file the report. I hesitated calling Hal back, because I knew he was waiting for a phone call, just not mine. Once I talked to Ray, I'd call him back and let him know what he needed to do. It was time that Ellie got over her qualms and took some action, or at least let Hal take some instead.

Telling Ray about Ben's weekend was almost as unsatisfactory as telling the Christian Friends at church. He let me talk for quite a while, not interrupting but just sipping his Americano. Despite wearing a bit of a frown while he listened he looked as gorgeous as ever. Instead of his usual work "uniform" of jeans and a sport coat with a white shirt, he had on khakis and a nice short-sleeved silk shirt in a tan-and-green print that accentuated the slight hazel tint to his golden-brown eyes. He'd settled me at the table with a kiss on the cheek and gotten our drinks before he sat down.

Mine was still largely full in front of me, the ice beginning to melt in my latte. While I seldom drank fancy coffee drinks at work at the Coffee Corner, I enjoyed them when somebody else made them. Once I finished telling Ray about Ben and Cai Li, with verbal detours to explain what was going on with Hal and Nicole, and what my friends had said this morning, I ran out of steam. Sipping the cool drink, I waited to hear what he'd say.

"Wow. That's a lot of information to digest at one time. And I hardly know what to tell you about Ben. Not having any kids myself, I don't know that I can make any pronouncements on somebody else's. I mean, he seems like a mature, solid kind of kid..."

"Whom you suspected was capable of murder just last fall," I put in, knowing it wouldn't earn me any points but still having to say it anyway. Suspecting Ben when Dot's contractor cousin was murdered during our apartment remodeling job was the one thing I held against Fernandez, and probably would for some time to come.

"I didn't suspect him seriously for any length of time, if you'll remember. You have to know that I was almost as relieved as you were when it turned out he wasn't a suspect. But he *was* close to the scene of the crime, and fit the description I had." If Ray ever gave up police work, he could definitely make it as a lawyer or a college lecturer, the man was so infallibly logical.

"But you did suspect him. And now you're saying that he's solid and mature. He's also not quite nineteen."

"Hey, when I was not quite nineteen I was almost finished with my associate's degree in criminal justice and on my way to the police academy as soon as they'd have me. If you would have asked me then, I'd have said I was ready to get married." His smile said he meant it, too.

"Yes, but you would have had the same problems Ben does now. No job, no place to live unless you wanted to bunk in with family, and dramatically lowered prospects to improve your situation unless one of you quit school and went to work."

"Wow, you've really thought this through, haven't you." He looked more serious now.

"I've thought it through because it's so familiar. I've lived it, Ray. And the last thing I want for my son is for him to make the same mistakes that his dad and I did." I fought back tears now, stinging behind my eyelids in equal parts of anger and frustration.

"Hey, nobody makes the exact same mistakes their parents make. They may make similar mistakes that are just as painful, but every generation puts its own unique stamp on their mistakes."

"Now that sounds like the voice of experience, too," I said, drawn away from my own problems for a moment.

"Yeah, kind of. I didn't make the same mistakes my parents made, but I've made some dandies. And to add to my own mistakes, in my line of work I see just about everybody's worst decisions. Nobody involves the Major Crimes Division because they made a good choice in life." He looked sad enough that I reached over and squeezed his hand.

"And that would lead us into our next topic of conversation. How does Hal file a missing person's report on his fiancée if she went to her bachelorette party and never came home?"

He grimaced. "Running away would be a particularly costly mistake, unless your ex is a lot worse than you've indicated. Has he already talked to the people she went out with?"

"Both of her bridesmaids say she got in her car about one and left. And her car is back at the house, so technically she came home but just didn't stay there."

"Has Hal talked to her family? Maybe they know something."

I shook my head. "No, and her mom and sister

have already come for the wedding and are giving Hal grief about filing a report. Can he do it if they object?"

"If she's an adult who's capable of looking after herself, they can't do much about it. He'd have as much right as they would to file the report. Why would they object, anyway?"

"I think they're afraid that somehow somebody will catch wind of this and then Nicole will slink home and be embarrassed by it all."

Ray made a sound that was remarkably like a growl. It certainly didn't sound like approval. "More likely they're afraid of embarrassment themselves. And if her dad's paying for some elaborate wedding, he's probably blowing a gasket by now."

That made me stop for a moment. "He's the one person in this whole mess who I haven't seen. Nobody says much about him, even. I know her mom isn't widowed or divorced, but where Mr. Barnes is, I have no idea."

"He's probably in the entertainment business somehow then, or a doctor. Or maybe he's part of my favorite profession, a lawyer. Something too busy to be bothered with the details of a daughter's wedding, anyway."

Ray was probably right. I made a mental note to ask Hal more about Nicole's dad. For that matter

Ben probably knew far more than I did. Ray took another drink of his cooling coffee, which probably had reached a temperature by now where I would have insisted that it get warmed up or put over ice, one or the other. How anybody drinks lukewarm coffee is beyond me, but Fernandez says he's so used to bad police department coffee that he'll drink better stuff at any temperature he can get it.

"So, filing a missing persons report, huh? First off, what you think you know about it is probably wrong."

I know I bristled a little. "Now why assume that?"

"Don't get huffy. Let me ask one question and see if you answer it right. If you do, go ahead and chew me out." I nodded agreement, not trusting myself to say much. "Okay, if you're filing on a voluntary missing adult like Nicole, how long do you have to wait?"

I tried not to look smug. "Twenty-four hours, right?"

He grinned. "Wrong. You've been watching too much TV again, Gracie. There's no waiting period anymore. If you're sure someone close to you is missing, you call the department dispatcher and she or he will send a patrol car, right then."

Okay, he had me there. "So when I woke up yesterday morning and found Ben's bed empty, I could have filed a report then?"

"You could have, not that it would have made you real popular with your son." Ray looked at his watch.

"Do you have to do a night shift or something?" He hardly ever checked the time when we were together.

"No, just dinner at my mom's." His smile was a bit weak. "I'd ask you to join me, but I don't want to get her hopes up. I'm old enough that if I take somebody to Mom's for dinner we better be talking about what to name the kids, or at least whether she prefers gold or platinum jewelry." The warm gaze that met mine had volumes of questions, almost all of which I wasn't ready to answer.

We talked for a few more minutes, he walked me to my car with a brief but warm hug and he drove away. I got into my car and sat in the parking lot for a minute, pondering my own long-term goals before I called Hal to tell him how to solve his short-term problem. In the end I decided I had too much to tell him, and pointed the car in the direction of Tuscany Hills one more time.

SIX

Halfway to Hal's my phone rang, and for a change I answered it in the car. Usually it takes an emergency for me to talk and drive at the same time, and I have a real problem with folks who do. When I saw that it was Hal I breathed a silent prayer that maybe Nicole had ended the drama and come home.

"Hal? Is she home?" I asked, trying to focus as much as I could on the road and not the phone and still listen to him while I drove.

"No. And you didn't call me back. No matter what Ellie says, I'm going to report Nicole missing."

"That's probably a good idea, as long as she's been gone. All you need to do is call the regular number for Ventura County Sheriff's Department, not 9-1-1, and Ray says they'll dispatch a patrol unit to your house as soon as possible."

"Okay. For a change having you date somebody

in law enforcement is a plus. I'll let you know when they've taken my report and I know something. Thanks, Gracie Lee."

I felt a wave of relief. "Does this mean you don't want me to come over?"

"Not now, at least. If anything happens, I'll call, okay? Right now I've got enough women to deal with as is, and sometime in the next two hours I'll add my mother to the mix." We said our goodbyes and I closed the phone, not anxious at all to go over there now. Dealing with Lillian has never been my favorite sport. Watching her take on Ellie Barnes could get rather ugly.

I went home, glad to have a bit of rest for the first time in the day. I kicked off my shoes, stretched out in the comfy chair in the living room and gave myself a rare treat of reading fiction for fun. An hour later the phone at the apartment rang. When I answered, Hal launched into a tirade without even saying hello. "Why didn't you tell me how invasive the questions were going to get, and how upsetting? I was nowhere near prepared for some of that stuff. I mean, they must automatically assume she's dead."

"Whoa. First off, I had no idea how invasive the questions might get because so far I've been lucky enough with our son that I've never had to file a report. And second, why do you say the police assume that Nicole is dead?"

"Because they had me sign these releases for dental records and health records and ghoulish things like that. Thank heavens, Ellie was here and could actually tell them who Nicole's family doctor and dentist were. She nearly went hysterical on me when she thought about why they'd need the information, but she gave it to them."

"I don't think you can assume anything from them asking for medical information. Knowing the sheriff's department they probably always do that to save time."

"Save time on what?"

"Coming back if they find a body that might match Nicole's description, or even a person who's alive but injured somehow, or has no identification, and then needing the records to identify them, or rule someone out. Wouldn't you rather that every available deputy is looking for Nicole instead of messing with details and paperwork?"

Hal sighed. "When you look at things that way, I'd agree. The deputy said that this would go in some kind of California computer system today, and something called the NCIS database that's national by tomorrow."

"Good. Maybe by then you won't need any of this because she'll show up, having a perfectly reasonable excuse as to why she's been gone." It was difficult to convince myself of that, but I could try.

"Right. I'm beginning to doubt that's going to happen. I've talked to Monica twice in addition to talking to Cat while you were here. Neither of them has heard from her, or seen her since one yesterday morning."

"Monica was the other person at the party?"

"Right. They all went back to her house after they went out, and she says Nicole was sober and heading for home the last time she saw her."

"That doesn't help much. I guess it gave you more to tell the police, though."

"For what that was worth. It didn't seem to impress the officer much. What he wanted most was the release of her medical records in case they needed them, and he wanted a current picture. At least I could give him that."

"I'm surprised that Ellie didn't argue over that, as well." She struck me as the type who might, given all the other squabbles they'd had.

"Oh, she did. In the end the officer wanted the picture I provided because it was more casual, and Ellie's was the posed shot they used for the newspapers for the engagement announcement."

Whatever newspapers that little item had gone in, it hadn't been the local *Star,* and so I hadn't been subjected to it. I decided not to say anything about that to Hal. He kept on talking anyway. "And I haven't even told you the best part yet. While the officer—in a marked patrol car of course—was still taking all the information, my mom and dad pull up in their rental car and Mom jumps out and starts having a fit."

"That had to be distressing. But I'm a little confused about something. Did you say your mom and dad got out of the same car?"

There was silence on the other end of the phone for long enough that I finally said, "Hal? Did we get cut off?"

"No, I'm still here. Just wondering why I hadn't told you the latest in that saga. My parents are back together."

"Wow." I wasn't sure I'd ever seen Roger and Lillian in the same room, so the thought of them as a couple was mind-boggling. "When did this happen?"

"Over the last few months. Mom was widowed in January, and Dad's current wife went to a high school reunion in March and never came home."

"Did she die, too, or find an old flame?"

"Found an old flame, sort of. I'm not going into details of what Dad told me, except that Rita is now living with her best friend from high school, Clara Jane."

"Ouch."

"Yeah, to say the least. He went over to Mom's one night to complain to somebody he didn't have to explain everything to. It seems they both decided they were too old to go through all the courting stuff again and too lonely to stay single. So he moved back home."

"That had to come as a surprise." Now maybe Hal having the dining room furniture made more sense. Knowing his mom, she probably wanted to get rid of some of the things she'd held on to that would have been in the house during her first marriage to Roger and make a fresh start. "So when did they make it official?"

The silence on the phone didn't last as long this time but still sounded pretty heavy. "Um, they haven't," Hal said eventually. "Dad's divorce from Rita isn't final yet. My parents are basically living in sin with each other."

Charming. Now I had even one more reason to avoid Hal's house for the next few weeks. His mother couldn't be in a good mood over this, and added to her driving up and seeing a police car in Hal's driveway, she'd be at ballistic level.

"Please, tell me you still want to handle this on your own," I said weakly.

"I certainly do. The only thing that would be worse than bringing you over here right now will be when Nicole walks in to explain where she has been."

It was a scene I didn't want to picture. Either Nicole didn't know Hal and his mother as well as I expected she would by now, or something terribly serious was still keeping her away. For Hal's sake I hoped it was a mild case of nerves mixed with a bit of ignorance on Nicole's part of the personalities involved. But given that she was a psychologist, and close to the Ph.D. level at that, this was beginning to sound like a disaster just waiting to play out.

"I'll keep praying for all of you, Hal. And I'm sorry it's been such an awful day." I really was sorry, too. Having things calm down with Hal meant we might be able to discuss Ben's situation in a quiet, reasonable manner. At this rate the kid would be married before his dad and I could sit down together to try to talk him out of it.

The rest of the evening was very quiet at the apartment. Ben came home from Cai Li's after dinner, still not talking much. With some urging he agreed that it would probably be a good idea for me to sit down with her parents and talk. "They're not as freaked out as you and Dad, maybe, but they're not real happy, either. It's not like any of you can do anything about it, you know."

I tried to breathe deeply and keep my response as calm as possible. "That's true, because you're both over eighteen. Neither of you need anybody's permission to get married. Still, that doesn't make me comfortable with the idea yet, and I've got a lot of questions to raise. Before you make any decisions or set any dates, there are a lot of things you need to talk over between the two of you, and with your parents, as well."

Ben sighed. "I know. But we really love each other, Mom. And we want to be together."

"I understand that part. I remember being young and in love. I also remember being broke, quitting school to earn money while your father finished his degree, and feeling very surprised to be having a baby before I turned twenty-one."

Ben's chin jutted out and his brow wrinkled. "Are you telling me you wish you hadn't had me?"

"No, I'd never say that. But your life would have been much easier if we'd waited a while. In all honesty, life would have been a lot easier for all three of us, and maybe you wouldn't have had to deal with your parents splitting up when you were so young. That's hard on any kid, and I wish we could have avoided it."

His posture relaxed a little. "It wasn't so bad, Mom, really. But Cai and I are different. And we'll work through things before we get married so we won't have problems and we won't get divorced. Your grandkids will have two parents who love them and love each other."

Grandchildren? I'd always known that as young as I had Ben I'd probably be a young grandmother, but I could certainly wait until several years after my fortieth birthday for that. Some people my age were still having children. Grandchildren weren't on my personal agenda yet.

Thinking about what Ben had said kept me up a lot longer than usual. That turned out to be a good thing for a change, because over an hour after I normally would have gone to bed my cell phone rang with Hal on the other end. After this many false alarms I didn't dare ask him if Nicole had come home. I just said hello and asked him what was up.

"Bad news and I'm scared." He sounded shaken and as though there were tears held back in a tight throat. That shocked me, because Hal had never been a guy who cried over anything. Even seventeen years ago when our daughter Emily died in the neonatal intensive care unit, he'd shed few tears.

He sounded as if he wanted to shed some now. "Tell me about it." A sinking sensation in my chest gave me a hint of what he might be telling me.

He took a deep breath. "The police sent someone to the door about fifteen minutes ago. When they put Nicole's information in the computer, it matched something from the other end of the county."

He said *something* instead of someone, which couldn't be good. "Do they want you to come and look at...a body?" It took a moment for me to say the word.

"They want someone to go to the county hospital in Ventura and look, yes. Apparently they don't usually do that anymore except with unidentified bodies, which is what they have."

"Oh, Hal. I'm so sorry."

"Hey, it could still be someone else. I'm holding out hope. All they would tell me was that they have the unidentified body of a young woman with dark hair. Ellie and I are arguing over who should go and when. I'd like to spare her the grief, especially since it might not be Nicole, but she's adamant she's going."

"Are you going tonight, or will you wait until morning?"

He made a strangled sound that wasn't words, just an expression of pain. "I don't know. If it's not Nicole it will be such a relief, after thinking that she might be dead. Even if she's still missing, that would be better than having this be her. If it is Nicole nobody will sleep tonight anyway, I guess." Talking it through made the decision for him. He took a deep breath. "Might as well do it."

I'd been silently praying for guidance while we talked but even I was surprised by the words that came out of my mouth next. "Do you want me to go with you?"

"Would you? I can't imagine going alone with

Ellie and Paige tonight. Or driving up there by myself, either."

Now that I felt committed to this project I thought a moment. "Do you still have that big black SUV?"

"Yeah, I do. It's been a pain since gas went past two-fifty a gallon, but I've got it."

"Then let me drive over there in my little car and take all of you to Ventura. You'll have to direct me to the hospital, but this would probably be better than any of the three of you driving."

He sighed. "You're right. As usual." There was a short, wry laugh on the other end of the phone. "Bet you never thought you'd hear me say that."

I didn't. But then I would have said half an hour ago that I wouldn't ever think of driving my ex-husband to the county morgue to possibly identify another woman, either. The older I get, the less I know for sure. If I get to be Dot Morgan's age I'll be totally clueless.

Halfway to Ventura I wanted to leave Nicole's sister by the side of the road. She had provided an unending stream of complaints and dialogue in an adenoidal whine. "This is so stupid. You know it's not going to be her. I mean, they said they found this girl naked washed up on the beach. That is so not anything Nicole would do."

"Paige, shut up," her mother finally snapped. "The whole goal of this trip is to make sure that whoever the police found isn't Nicole. And we all know it wouldn't be like her to go skinny-dipping in the ocean in June. Nobody in their right mind would do that."

Ellie was right there. The Pacific in June reminded me of the one time I'd gone to Chicago in July and tried to wade in Lake Michigan—ice-cold even with bright sunshine playing off the surface. And I'd finally gotten used to the fact that early June wasn't a very sunny time in Southern California anyway. We have this stuff called "June gloom" that means clouds and even fog and cool temperatures almost every morning that burns off by about ten. Dressing in layers is a summer art form around here. No one who had grown up near here would take a midnight dip in the ocean for any length of time without a wetsuit.

Her mother's sharp words made Paige subside for a while. She still grumbled and muttered behind me, but nothing was loud enough for me to really make out the words. For now that was a blessing. I had a few small things to be thankful for on this trip, the most important being that Ben had stayed home to sleep. Staying up as many hours as he had had finally caught up with him. Even his wish to be a support to his dad, and to me, was canceled out by exhaustion.

Now that Paige had pulled this spoiled brat act for miles, I felt relieved that Ben wasn't here to see it. He was also too young to face any of what we might see at the county morgue tonight. No matter that he argued he was a mature young man ready to get married, he was still my kid. Regardless of who was there at the morgue to be identified, this would be a rough night for everyone involved.

Beside me in the front passenger seat, Hal gripped the armrest so tightly I was afraid it might come off in his hand. He hadn't said anything through Paige's constant commentary or Ellie's outburst, either. I almost felt like reaching over and patting his hand. If the 101 wasn't so dark I would have considered it. As is, we didn't need to add running off the road to the disasters of the past day. Besides, I couldn't imagine Ellie letting me touch her daughter's fiancé without another tirade. She probably couldn't fathom that after these many years of separation all I wanted to offer Hal was sympathy for a rough situation.

The first time Hal spoke was to give me directions on what exit to take off the freeway. Even though he hadn't been to the county before, he had good instructions from the sheriff's deputy who had come to his house earlier.

At this time of night we parked in a half-empty lot at the hospital and were directed through the emergency department, the only doors open, to the less-than-cheery facility that housed the county morgue. A woman with short red hair and a no-nonsense disposition introduced herself as a county death investigator on the medical examiner's staff and proceeded to talk to Hal and Ellie while Paige and I hung back a little. We didn't talk to each other.

In the quiet I could hear the investigator telling Ellie and Hal that nothing had been found on the body except a pair of pink underwear and a thin gold chain necklace. "But what about her engagement ring? Or the pearl stud earrings her grandmother gave her? Surely if this was Nicole she would have been wearing those," Ellie argued.

"Maybe the police didn't explain things to you very well," the investigator said softly. "This body has apparently been in the water for a day or two. Being in the ocean for that long would have removed most jewelry. It will also make identification by sight rather difficult."

A shudder ran through me as I considered her words. Maybe this would convince Ellie to let Hal look for both of them to save her any possible grief. Paige had apparently heard everything, as well. She turned away and seemed to be searching for something. She walked briskly over to a desk across the room in the waiting area that probably served as an office in the daytime and, leaning over a wastebasket, she spit out a wad of gum.

"Miss, if you're going to be ill I can show you where the ladies' room is just around the corner."

Paige looked up at her with fright in her eyes and gulped convulsively. "Not if it's closer to… her…or it…or them or whatever. I'll just stay here. I'll be okay." With her eyes wide with fear and her face as pale as her hair, she looked like the kid she was, not much older than Ben.

"No, there's a set of restrooms outside the door there, away from our facility." The examiner pointed through the glass doors with the county medical examiner's logo on them to the darkened hallway beyond.

I felt a flash of pity for the kid, no matter how aggravating she'd been earlier. She was scared and worried, and had probably been filling the silence before just to keep from panicking.

"Come on, I'll go with you," I said, motioning toward the hallway. She didn't look like someone who would welcome me taking her hand. But she seemed grateful for the company and the reason to leave this room. I had to admit that going out to the restroom with Paige was far preferable to staying with Hal and her mother.

I stood outside the restroom door, listening to her pacing inside. It took her fifteen minutes to calm down and want to go back to the morgue office. When we did, we were just in time to see Ellie and Hal come out into the lobby again, arguing as they came.

SEVEN

"That is not my daughter." Ellie's face was grim as she strode out ahead of everyone else. Her face looked as ashen as her hair and she trembled, but her voice was firm and sure.

"Now Ellie, how can you say that? I don't want to believe that it's Nicole, either, but obviously that's her. That's her necklace, her underwear, and the hair is the right color and cut." Hal couldn't look at Ellie while he spoke. He looked back to the morgue employee, as if for validation.

She put a hand lightly on Ellie's shoulder only to have it shrugged off immediately. Still, Ellie stood still to listen to her. "I tried to warn you that being in the ocean for many hours can make a person almost unrecognizable, Mrs. Barnes." Her voice was soft and apologetic. "If you still have doubts..."

Ellie wheeled around on the hapless woman. "I

don't have any doubts at all. That is not Nicole. She's never been that fat, or that pale. And she certainly doesn't have any bruises like that girl, unless *he* put them there." She flashed Hal a purely venomous look.

Crossing the room, she grabbed her remaining daughter by the wrist. "Come on, Paige. We're going outside where I can call your father. He'll get this sorted out with some *competent* medical people." The last was spit out over her shoulder, glaring while still dragging Paige out the door. Before anyone could respond, Ellie left with Paige in tow.

I looked at Hal and the death investigator, but still didn't say anything for a moment or two. There didn't seem to be anything for me to say at this point; I hadn't seen the body, and wasn't sure I would have been able to identify Nicole if I had. Hal watched Ellie leave, and then turned toward the morgue employee. "She's wrong, isn't she?" His voice sounded soft and sorrowful.

"I'm afraid so. All the information you've given the sheriff's department suggests that the young woman in there is your fiancée, Mr. Harris. Denial is a natural reaction to this kind of crushing news, though. And sometime tomorrow we'll be able to verify the identity of our victim one way or another when we have Ms. Barnes's dental records. Until then her mother will probably remain convinced that we don't have her daughter."

Hal looked at the floor. "How long will it be before we know how she died?"

"There will be preliminary autopsy reports by late tomorrow. But any toxicology screens will take much longer. It will more than likely be a few days before we have any definite cause of death."

"Once you identify her you'll probably want to talk to the two women Nicole went out with Friday night. I know they planned to go to a bar, so don't be surprised to find alcohol in her system. Probably not much, though. She isn't...wasn't what anybody would call a drinker."

"I'll get that information when we need it, Mr. Harris. But first we need to identify her to everybody's satisfaction. Then we can come up with a cause of death."

Hal nodded. "Okay. Thank you, Dr...."

"Halloran. And it's not doctor, just plain Meg. I'll call you and Mrs. Barnes both the moment I know something for sure."

Hal thanked her again and we left, looking for Ellie and Paige. Unless they had somehow called a cab, they couldn't have gotten very far. Outside it felt damp with fog rolling in from the ocean. Not too far from the SUV we found Nicole's family. They had gone outside where Ellie was talking loudly into a cell phone, gesturing broadly with her free hand as she paced in the pool of light cast by a parking lot light pole.

"No, of course it isn't her. It can't be her. This woman was found nearly naked on the beach, rolled in with the tide. And besides, Paul, it couldn't have possibly been Nicole." Her voice dropped lower and she turned away from us. "This girl was bloated and fat."

There was a long silence after that. Ellie's shoulders began to shake and finally she choked out a few words. "No. I don't want to hear any of that. None of your medical talk. It's too grotesque. Just get up here in the morning and straighten this out, will you?" There was a pause while Ellie kept pacing. "So what if you have a full schedule, this is *your* daughter we're talking about."

The emphasis she put on the "your" instead of the "daughter" made me think. Was this one of those families where the parents had each claimed one of the children for their own? I'd seen that before among friends and acquaintances, and it made for a lot of discord. It was another thing to ask Hal at a quieter time.

After a moment or two more, Ellie flipped her phone closed and turned around, drawing the back of one perfectly manicured hand across her cheek, wiping away tears. "I guess we're ready to go back to the house now." She looked pointedly at me and I realized I had the keys to the vehicle and needed to let everybody in.

There was almost nothing said the entire trip back. For a while Hal turned on the radio, but the stations were either droning sports talk or playing music that sounded much too cheery for the current circumstances. After a while he turned it off in disgust, making me wish I'd brought one of my CDs from the car. I had no idea how Ellie would have felt about Christian music at this point, but I certainly could have used some assurance. Instead I concentrated on getting us to Hal's without incident on the foggy roads.

When we got to the house Ellie and Paige came out of the back seat so fast they could have been jet-propelled. They were at the door to the guesthouse and inside without another word to either of us.

"Well. So much for any family support." Hal sounded exhausted, and I wondered if he'd really gotten any sleep since yesterday morning.

"Do you want me to stay for a while, or go home? If there's anything you need help with..."

Hal waved me away, the ghost of a smile playing across his face for a moment. "Thanks, Gracie Lee, but I think I'd rather be alone right now. With any luck my parents have gone to bed and slept through any noise we made coming back. They're old enough that travel wears them out now. That's why I didn't dare suggest that Dad drive us to the county hospital."

I nodded, knowing all too well what he meant. Being in the middle of a generational sandwich had its ups and downs even without a runaway bride. "I hope you're right. If she's awake, your mom will be a basket case."

"I know. But I don't see any lights on in there, so I'm betting they're asleep. It's funny…part of me wants the company, but the other part is still grasping at the faint hope that maybe Ellie's right. It's so unlikely that I'm not sure I can keep that feeling if I talk about all this too much."

"I guess it's a possibility that the person they found wasn't Nicole." Not a big one, but I had to admit there was a chance that Nicole was still out there somewhere alive, just another young woman having second thoughts about a wedding.

"We'll all know for sure tomorrow." Hal gave a sigh that came from deep in his chest. "I'll call you then. And this time I promise, I'll call."

"Thanks." Hal watched me get in my car and start the engine before he unlocked his back door and went into the house. Those Southern manners were so deeply ingrained that even under stress like he faced tonight, he still acted the gentleman.

I wish I could have said the same about Ray.

Driving home to the apartment had me thinking angry thoughts about the detective. Obviously he had to have known what we just found out. With working the major crimes unit, any unidentified body would be reported to them. He knew Nicole was missing and I didn't understand why he hadn't let me know. I almost called him when I got home to tell him what I thought of his silence, but in the end my better judgment won out and I let the man sleep uninterrupted. I'd be just as aggravated tomorrow morning.

Ben looked up from the computer when I came in. "Hey, Mom. Was it…"

"Nicole? Your dad thinks so, her mom doesn't. But the death investigator at the morgue seems to side with your dad. So, yes. I have to say it probably is."

"Wow. Let me sign off with Cai so we can talk." He turned back to the screen, typed rapidly and sent a last instant message and shut down the machine. He insisted on making me sit down on the sofa while he made me a cup of chamomile tea and asked questions about what had happened at the morgue.

Having my son be this solicitous of my feelings only one day after he nearly drove me to panic had me close to tears. I imagined for a moment how I'd feel if I had been the one having to identify a child at the morgue tonight. Maybe Ellie's denial wasn't so strange, after all. Perhaps in her situation I'd be putting off the worst news, even if I knew it was inevitable, for as long as I could. The hug I gave Ben before we each went to our room that night was tight and clingy. He didn't object, and I thanked God for that.

Sleep didn't come easily. For a while I wasn't sure it would come at all. But once I went to sleep Sunday night I slept for an uninterrupted eight hours, not waking Monday morning even when Buck fed the dogs and did all the morning chores at the kennels outside my bedroom windows. Now that I didn't help him with that work every morning I didn't automatically wake up when it was time to do the job. As I had picked up more responsibilities during the last bit of graduate school, I'd let Frankie Collins take over that set of duties.

Frankie, a solidly built thirteen-year-old, needed the male companionship Buck could provide since the death of his father last year, and his family welcomed the money, as well. Due to a host of problems he and his two little sisters were living with an aunt and uncle. School would finish up soon for the Collins kids and I'd probably be seeing more of Frankie around the place during the summer. His uncle's house was close enough to

Dot and Buck's kennels that he rode his bike over to help most mornings, then had a quick breakfast with the Morgans and headed on to middle school. I realized with a start that he would be in high school in the fall. Everybody's kids were growing up, not just mine.

Ben wasn't up yet, but to appease me he'd left his bedroom door open just a bit so that I could see that he was there and asleep. While I made coffee quietly I pondered what to do next with his situation. I still didn't think that marrying at nineteen was the right thing for him to do. Cai Li was a great kid, but that was the problem; they were both such kids that even another year would probably change their perspective on marriage. Now how could I convince him of that without alienating him?

I didn't find any answers to my questions staring into my cup of coffee. Even my morning Bible study didn't give me a definite answer on how to proceed. But by the time I'd finished my study and coffee it was just late enough that I knew Ray would either be getting his morning caffeine fix on the way to work or already be at his desk. Of course that assumed some other emergency hadn't put him out in the field.

Still, I dialed his cell phone and amazingly he answered instead of it switching directly into his voice mail. That stumped me for a minute because

I expected to vent at a recording and here he was in person, sounding terribly alert and cheery.

Later in the day I might have been more tactful, but early morning wasn't my best time. "Why didn't you tell me that you'd found a body that was probably Nicole?"

"I didn't find anything, actually. The call came in to the medical examiner's office straightaway." Smooth, I thought. He managed to stay totally truthful without giving any answer to the question.

"You know exactly what I mean. And thanks to not being informed, I got to drive Hal and Nicole's mother and sister to the county morgue without any warning whatsoever."

He was quiet for a minute. "Honestly, I didn't know you had gotten that involved in all this, Gracie. I mean, he's your ex-husband and all. Why is he turning to you?"

"Because he didn't have anybody else to turn to except Ben, and he's way too young to deal with this. That or his parents, and they're too old. Nicole's family is in total denial over this and sniping at Hal, and my ex-in-laws just got in late yesterday."

"Okay, now I'm even more confused. I know you've said before that Hal's parents divorced more than twenty years ago. Aren't they married to other people, or did you mean that they're traveling as a group of four?"

Leave it to Ray to pick up on that right away. The question might be a diversionary tactic to make me wander off the main issue, but I felt I should give him an answer. It didn't make any sense not telling him the truth while I complained about him not telling me what he knew. "It's complicated. Lillian is widowed, Roger's in the middle of a divorce and they're back together again anyway, giving Ben one more example of how not to live your life in a relationship."

"Yet another reason to stay out of all of this," Ray said, sounding like the voice of sanity. The man was very close to driving me over the edge. The last thing I wanted right now was a detached voice of reason.

"It is way, way too late for me to stay out of this, as you put it." I wasn't even sorry that he could probably hear the anger in my voice. "Once Ben announced his engagement on the same day that Nicole disappeared, that was the end of any chance for me not to be involved."

"Surely you could handle Ben's problems without being around your ex-husband so much. I'm not even sure this much contact is healthy. No, scratch that. I know this much contact is unhealthy and I'm upset that you're involved."

"Why? And who says your opinion counts in this situation?" Okay, now I was raising my voice on the phone, which was not cool at all. But Ray was pulling the machismo thing, telling me what to do, and I wasn't having any, thank you very much.

"This isn't just personal. As a member of the team investigating this incident as long as it remains a suspicious death, I definitely have some say in this. If this turns out to be murder, Gracie, I'd like to point out that the two most likely possibilities for a young woman Nicole's age are that she was either murdered by someone very close to her *like her fiancé* or a serial killer got her. In either case poking your nose into this could get you into deep trouble."

"Statistics can say anything you want them to if you work hard enough at it. And I'm upset that you'd automatically suspect Hal of murder, especially when we don't even know it was murder yet, much less that the body is definitely Nicole."

"Do you doubt that the body that washed up on the beach is Nicole Barnes?"

The silence filled the space between us, cold and hard until I finally answered him. "Honestly? Not really."

"Well, add that to the fact that Nicole's car was parked in her own driveway when she went missing and it still argues to those two possibilities. Either Hal staged this to look like a disappearance, or someone got to her between the car and her back door without there being signs or sound of a struggle."

Put that way, stepping away from the personal details and into the facts as Ray probably saw them, I had to admit it looked bad for Hal. "Okay, you have several good points there," I conceded. "But it's still too late for me to back out all together. Ben's pretty shaken up about all of this, and I still haven't resolved anything with him and Cai Li about marriage. And to do that I need to have some cooperation from his father."

"Who says you are going to resolve anything? This just might be one of those issues where you don't get your way, Gracie."

This conversation was sliding downhill rapidly. "You know what? Forget that I called. I'm sorry that I interrupted your day. Maybe we'll talk later, as in a few weeks from now."

The one problem with modern phones as opposed to the old corded kind of my childhood is that now no matter how hard you slam them down they don't make the same sound, that ghost of a chime indicating finality. That sound used to lend such a serious note to the end of a conversation. Somehow putting a cordless handset in its base or flipping a cell phone closed just doesn't provide the same release.

Still, it was the best I could do. Ray might be

right about Ben, but he wasn't right about Hal. I just knew that in my heart. And he wasn't right about me staying away from this investigation, whether or not it turned out to be murder as he hinted might be the case. Chances were good that the body was Nicole, but there was nothing that Ray could tell me that would convince me that Hal had killed his fiancée.

By the time I finished talking to Ray on the phone and hanging up on him, I'd apparently made enough noise to wake up Ben. He emerged from his room wearing ratty pajama pants with sleep in his eyes. It was beyond my comprehension that someone was looking forward to marrying the vision in front of me, but I kept my thoughts to myself there. He wasn't any more of a morning person than I was, and I had a prejudice against his skinny but fashionable goatee. At least it was trimmed these days and his hair, though a bit long, was neat.

"Sorry if I woke you. I didn't mean to get that loud."

He gave me a wry smile. "Must have been Dad or Detective Fernandez on the phone. They're the only people I can think of besides me that get you that riled up."

"The detective. Dad hasn't called back this morning, which means he hasn't heard anything yet from the medical examiner."

"I feel really sorry for him." Ben stretched and sat down in the living room armchair. "This has to be a horrible thing for him to go through."

"It may get more horrible. What I was arguing with Fernandez about was his statement that if Nicole has been murdered, your dad is very high on the suspect list."

Ben shook his head. "Not possible. I don't even want to talk about that."

"I know. That's what I told him, too. But he's a detective and doesn't know your dad like we do. And speaking of knowing someone well, it's time I started getting to know Cai Li's parents. How about we set something up later today for the moms to get together at least?"

Ben rolled his eyes. "I figured you were going to ask about that soon. Maybe I'd rather talk about Dad and Nicole, after all."

"Nope, too late for that. If you're talking about making me somebody's mother-in-law, it's time I met her parents. What does her mom do, so I can work around her schedule and mine?"

"She manages a nail salon on the other side of Rancho Conejo. Monday's usually her day off, so maybe you can get together." He looked resigned, like someone contemplating the firing squad. "If this is going to happen, might as well get it going."

I couldn't agree with him more. Maybe we

could all take our minds off the troubles at Hal's house with something that would move us in a more positive direction. By noon I found myself sitting in Mai Pham's sunny yellow kitchen drinking tea while we shared stories that our kids would probably rather we didn't.

EIGHT

Mai Pham gave me an idea of what Cai Li might be like in twenty years, and I liked what I saw. The confident, quick-moving woman who served me tea and insisted on putting a plate of cookies on the table before she sat down gave the air of knowing what she was about.

Her inky hair swung in a chic cut around her shoulders and her eyes glittered with almost the same shade of ebony. Her unlined face made her look barely old enough to have a child Cai Li's age, and I doubted she'd had any kind of work done. Maybe she had married as young as I had. If that was the case, what did she think about the kids marrying this young? "We give our children traditional names to keep the old ways alive. But they are American." She said the last word, in her lightly accented English, with mixed resignation and pride, shaking her head. "In Vietnam, Cai would listen to her parents about getting married. Some people her age still use matchmakers there. Here there is no asking, just telling."

"I know what you mean. Ben just came home after they stayed up all night together and said they were engaged." I took a sip of the green jasmine tea with its earthy notes of grass and flowers and looked at the mug Mai had put in front of me. Like several at my house, it proclaimed the owner a middle school honor roll student. I wondered if it belonged to Cai or one of the two younger brothers she'd mentioned. "We all want the same thing for them. Just more chances than we had ourselves."

Mai nodded. "When we came here, we were refugees. Teenagers, we go to work right away. My children became American citizens first, then their father and me. Duc worked two jobs, went to night school, later took the CPA exam. After that, my turn to go to school. I just learn more English and some business. We work hard, so our children don't have to work so hard."

That had such a familiar ring to it. "Ben's father and I are divorced. You probably know that from Ben." Mai nodded. "We married as young as these two want to, and it was a mistake. Neither one of us was ready."

Her answering smile only lifted one corner of

her mouth. "When we marry, Duc is twenty-two, I am twenty-four. Old for Vietnam, still young for here."

I revised my estimate of her age upward a bit, doing the math in my head. Looking around the plant-filled kitchen with a prep area and breakfast nook about the size of the entire living, dining and kitchen areas of my apartment, it was clear all the Phams' hard work had paid off. "Does it make you unhappy that the kids want to marry so young?"

"A little. But it is good they are free to do it. And I understand, this is the Christian way. Duc and me, we are more Buddhist than Christian. Sometimes Cai Li takes me to her church. It is a good place. Mike and Doug like to go with her." She wrinkled her nose slightly as she said the names. "Her brothers, we name them Minh and Duc. But they go to school, they come home Mike and Doug. Cai Li keeps her Vietnamese name, but falls in love with an American boy."

She drank some tea and picked up a cookie, then put it down. "Your family. Do they care Cai Li is Vietnamese?"

Her question made me speechless for a moment. I thought before I answered. "I don't care. She's bright, funny and beautiful. I wonder what someone as mature as she is sees in Ben sometimes. Hal, Ben's father, doesn't seem to care or notice, either.

I don't know how Hal's mother and father will feel about it. They're from the South, from Tennessee. His father is a Korean war veteran."

Mai nodded again. "Duc's mother live with his sister in Westminster. First time one of her grandson brings home blond surfer girl, she nearly have a stroke. Now things are better. When she is here for Mother's Day, she met Ben and she even like his…" Obviously struggling for the word in English, she drew fingers over her chin.

"That goatee? If your mother-in-law likes that, she's one step ahead of me. I'd be thrilled if he shaved it off."

We laughed together then, and I began to get the feeling that whatever the kids finally worked out, they just might be okay. Okay, so none of us was thrilled by the fact that our nineteen- and twenty-year-old kids wanted to get married. But obviously they'd been raised right and it looked as though we were just going to have to trust the Lord on this one. Handing things like this over to God was still the hardest part of my maturing faith. Maybe it always would be.

When I got back to the apartment Ben was still there, which surprised me. He had told me he was going to start looking for a summer job and I'd expected to find him gone. But there he was, sitting on one of the stools at the counter on the pass-through into the kitchen. When I came into the room, relief washed over his face.

"I'm glad you're home. Dad called and I didn't know what to do. I knew you were at Cai's and I didn't want to call you there, but he sounded really upset."

I knew before I asked what had probably happened, but I had to ask anyway. "Did they hear from the medical examiner?"

"Yeah, they did. Even worse, Dad says Nicole's father came up and looked at the body and everything, and he agrees with the police. It's definitely Nicole that they found, Mom. And Dad says the sheriff's department people told him not to go anyplace without telling them."

Ben's grim expression said that he knew what that meant. He had his own brush with being a suspect in Frank Collins' murder in November, even though the suspicion against him was mercifully brief. After that, he knew what the words "don't leave town" meant.

"Ben, they pretty much have to say that. Until they know how Nicole died and who might have been involved, they're going to be suspicious of the people closest to her. You and I know that the idea that your dad would harm Nicole in any way is pretty far-fetched. But the medical examiner and the sheriff's department don't know that until they do more investigation. More than likely this is all a tragic accident of some kind and they'll find that out quickly. The next couple weeks will be hard on everybody, but we can pray that whatever happens will bring out the truth and bring it out quickly."

Ben swallowed hard and nodded. My heart ached for him. While I wanted him to be more mature, this wasn't the kind of experience I had in mind to help mature him. Even if Hal and I had been at each other's throats over our divorce for the last fifteen years, which we hadn't, this wasn't a trial I'd wish on him, or even my worst enemy. When I said that the next few weeks would be hard on everybody, what I didn't spell out for Ben was that it would be as hard on me as anyone else. If the medical examiner thought this really was a murder, my ex-husband would be high on the list of suspects and Ray Fernandez would be one of the main people trying to prove him guilty.

It took another hour for me to figure out what to say to Hal when I called him back. In between I consoled Ben a little and tried to assure him that Mai Pham and I had gotten along well with each other. I couldn't tell him what he wanted to hear, which was that we both thought our kids planning a wedding was a great idea. But at least I could tell him that Mai seemed like a really nice person and both moms could agree that we really liked each other's kids.

To get a smile out of Ben I told him what Mai said about Cai Li's grandmother and his beard. He grinned, saying that he had been making sure the goatee was neatly trimmed all the time because both Cai Li and her grandmother's opinions were important to him. "I know what your opinion is, Mom. But as long as Cai Li likes this," he said, stroking the scrawny blond fur covering his chin, "it's going to stay."

I patted his shoulder, marveling again how much I had to reach up to do it. "I know you didn't grow it to impress me, son. And I'd be foolish to think you'd shave it off to please me, either." Especially when his lady love liked the awful thing. That was the difference between Ben and his father at the same age; when Hal's mother had complained about the way he dressed early in our marriage, he went back to the prep button-downs I hated. Lillian had always had more influence with Hal than I had, which made for a lot of strife. I couldn't very well fault Ben for the very behavior I'd told my Christian Friends group I had wanted to see from his father.

Right now I felt like calling one or more of those friends. Probably any of them would be able to help me call Hal and say the right thing. But Linnette would be upset to hear about Nicole's death, and almost everybody else was at work or otherwise busy. This time I'd have to rely on prayer and good common sense to get me through.

In the end things were far easier than I thought they would be because Hal wasn't answering his phone. Getting his answering machine made it easy to tell him how sorry I felt, and how I'd be there if he wanted to talk later. Once that was done I picked up the Want Ads out of the local newspaper and went through them seeing if anything struck me as a likely possibility for Ben. When I showed him my circled "finds" he shook his head.

"That's pretty old school, Mom. These days you get on line to find jobs. I've been working on it most of the day, and one of my suite-mates said he'd put in a good word at the office supply store where he's been working since senior year in high school."

It sounded like a good plan and I told him so. "It beats being a camp counselor or mowing lawns, anyway. I'm going to go pick up the application and try to get an interview this week."

I resisted asking him if the job paid enough to support him, because I knew it didn't. If he got the job his first paycheck would bring that home far more clearly than I ever could.

When my phone rang about six in the evening I didn't bother to see who was calling before I picked it up.

So Linnette's voice on the other end surprised me a little; I figured it might be Hal returning my call and I told her so, filling her in on the news about Nicole. "Hmm. Playa del Sol sure doesn't waste any time."

"What do you mean?"

"I mean they've already had someone from community relations call and tell me to be prepared for a different person to lead our therapy group on Wednesday. The voice mail I got said there would be a letter in the mail soon explaining everything, but they wanted to keep their clients from being surprised by the change."

"Hey, I can imagine some of Nicole's patients will be really thrown for a loop over hearing this news." As I talked, a picture of Zoë flashed in my mind. She would probably blame the loss of her therapist on the evil forces she saw everywhere. I could only imagine what sorts of damage the death of a therapist could cause for a person as unstable as Zoë appeared.

Linnette sounded a little confused. "The one odd thing is that Nicole had already told us we'd have someone else leading the group this week anyway. She said another doctoral student who needed the clinical hours, her friend, Monica something, would be leading the sessions because of the upcoming wedding."

"So the hospital could have waited until next

week to say anything," I said, more thinking out loud than anything.

"Probably two or three weeks. I mean, even therapists take a honeymoon, don't they?"

"I'd have to think so. That part of the plans never came up when I've been talking with Hal." When my shoulders sagged a bit with relief, I realized I'd been holding them tight and stiffly for quite some time. It was good to realize that I hadn't heard every detail of Hal's problems and planning. Maybe he had at least one other friend to lean on so that he could spread his troubles around.

The name Linnette mentioned rang a bell. "I wonder if it's the same Monica who was the third person at the bachelorette party." I told her about Hal's statements so far and his phone calls from Monica. "She apparently told Hal and the police that the three of them went back to her house after their partying. The last either she or Cat claims to have seen of Nicole was her getting in her car and leaving Monica's condo."

"If it's the same person, I wonder why they've got her leading our group," Linnette mused. "She's probably almost as upset as Nicole's family about her being missing, and now knowing that she's dead." Linnette sighed. "I can tell that this is going to be a real tough group session Wednesday. How much do you think they'll tell us?"

"I have no idea. They'll probably be fairly up-front about her death, I'd assume, because you know this will make the papers. Even if it's an accidental death, the police reports from last night about picking up an unidentified body should generate some interest among the news outlets."

Saying it to Linnette was the first time I'd thought about that, and it made me resolve to be much more careful about answering the phone. Harris is a fairly common last name, but if Sam Blankenship at the Ventura County *Star* caught wind that I had any involvement in a case like this, however far removed, he'd be calling me any old time. Sam wasn't a bad guy, and so far he'd been more than fair in his dealings with me as he'd reported his way up the ladder on the crime beat. He'd used his writing about my late husband Dennis's murder to interest editors in moving him out of covering just features, and I knew his story about Frank Collins was one of several that made him a regular contributor to crime news around the county. Nicole might have been found too late last night to make today's paper, but we could all count on seeing something in the *Star* tomorrow.

It was actually Sam's article the next morning that kept me from having to ask Hal any more questions about Nicole for a while. Like any good reporter, Sam had found as much information as possible, including wringing all that he could out of someone at the medical examiner's office. I had to imagine it wasn't Meg Halloran; she didn't strike me as the type to talk to reporters more than she had to. Tuesday, another gloomy June morning found me sipping coffee and reading the front page of the *Star*'s local section.

What I read made me more than a little uneasy. My mind raced as I read, trying to figure out how to explain part of the information for Ben. According to the preliminary autopsy report that Sam quoted, there appeared to be high levels of alcohol and perhaps several drugs in Nicole's system, and even more depressing, there was water in her lungs. The water was an obvious thing that would need little more study except to verify that it was seawater or not. The alcohol and drug screens could take weeks, according to Sam's sources.

Ben got up and I told him all of this, to which he responded in confusion, as I expected him to, over why I looked glum. "Water in her lungs will more than likely make the medical examiner's final ruling suicide or homicide," I explained to him.

"Does that mean she drowned?" Ben looked solemn, and I could tell that he was working through in his mind what that might mean for the suspicion falling on his dad.

"It does, or at least it means that drowning was part of what caused her death. In any case, it definitely means she was alive when she went into the water." And it posed a few questions that I'm sure Ray or whoever was heading up the investigative team for the sheriff's department would be asking.

How did a young woman whose car was in her driveway at home get into the ocean at least seven or eight miles away from there in the middle of the night? She obviously had to have help of some kind, whether it was someone who transported her there willingly or someone disposing of what they thought was a body. I couldn't imagine Hal could do either, but convincing a trained law-enforcement expert of that would certainly be an uphill battle.

The number of problems all this raised for my ex-husband made me feel sorry for him. Just days ago he'd been facing what ought to have been one of the happiest days of his life. Now there was sadness in front of him, and plenty of contention. Instead of a wedding there would be a funeral, and the money Hal's parents had probably planned to use for a big rehearsal dinner might go for a good criminal lawyer instead. "Do you think they'll arrest Dad?" Ben asked.

I have always been as honest as possible with him, and I didn't intend to start lying now. "It might come to that. For your sake, and for his and your grandparents, I pray it doesn't happen. But I've seen enough police investigation by now to know how this might all look to the county sheriff's department." And along with praying for Hal and his family, I'd pray for Ray, too. I'd pray for good judgment and discernment, with the hope that if someone did have to arrest my ex-husband, Ray Fernandez wasn't the one to do it.

NINE

"I imagine you could start driving yourself to your therapy sessions any old time," I remarked to Linnette as we headed down the freeway toward Playa del Sol.

"Pretty soon," she said, settling her latte back in the cup holder. "But with all the commotion going on with Nicole's death, I'd just as soon have company this week. Besides, I thought you might want to take a look at everything one more time."

"I do, but quietly. If Ray finds out that I've done anything but drive you to your group therapy session and back, he'll blow a gasket."

"I hadn't thought about it that way. I hope I don't get you in trouble just by asking for another ride." Linnette sounded worried. Little things like this told me my friend wasn't back to one hundred percent normal yet, although she was definitely on the way there. She's usually plenty considerate of others' feelings, but not in a way that puts herself down. I waved off her concern.

"I've brought plenty of books to study with, so even if the detective shows up on the job, he'll see that I'm not 'snooping around,' as he calls it." To back up my statement I spread my books out on my bench in the courtyard as soon as possible once we got into Playa del Sol and Linnette headed toward her therapy session.

I wondered if Zoë was there, and how she'd handle the news that Nicole wasn't coming back. Linnette seemed to need all the stability she could get right now, so somebody like Zoë, who had far more challenges, could be even more disturbed by her therapist's death.

I wondered if Monica or someone in charge at the facility would even tell Nicole's patients that her absence was due to death. Nothing Linnette had gotten from the hospital had said Nicole was dead—she only knew that from me and the newspaper. How did privacy laws work in that respect? I made a mental note to ask someone about that if I got a chance.

That chance came sooner than I expected. Ten minutes later, while I was deep into my reading, a tall figure stood next to me. When I looked up I saw it was Catalina, the nurse I'd seen leading Zoë another day. "Hi. Am I in somebody's way?"

I couldn't think of a reason for her to stand by me quietly.

"No, not at all." Her long blond hair was pulled back in a more severe style today, and her eyes were red-rimmed, as if she'd been crying. "I hate to interrupt you, but the last time you were here Nicole told me who you were, and I wanted to talk to you."

My common sense told me that whatever she wanted to talk about would be something that Ray would go ballistic over. I could almost hear the lecture he'd give about possible witnesses to a crime, or even murder suspects and how I should stay uninvolved here. Common sense is not always my strong point. When it's a battle between that and caring for people, the caring wins every time. Catalina looked like she needed somebody to care right now.

I cleared books away to make an empty spot on the bench. "So what did Nicole tell you, anyway?"

She looked around as if checking for her supervisor, then sat down beside me. "That you were Hal's ex-wife, and you were really cool with everything. It helped her a lot, I think. She was so nervous about being a stepmother, especially to somebody not much younger than her sister."

"I can understand that. But surely that isn't why you wanted to talk to me." Okay, I couldn't help saying more than I should to her. Maybe I'd be truly fortunate and Ray wouldn't show up here today.

"Not exactly. It's just that I know you've probably got a lot of contact with Hal, and with Nicole's family. She's got a desk full of stuff here and nobody's even started cleaning out her cubicle or anything yet. It's kind of creepy, seeing all her stuff still there like she's coming back any old time."

I could appreciate that. When my former husband Dennis died he'd left all kinds of belongings for me to deal with. Of course I'd dealt with a lot of them after the serious auto accident five months before he died. But even after all that he'd had a nightstand at the board-and-care home where he'd spent his final months and a few boxes of stuff stored at his mom's house that still had to be gone through. For someone who'd had no warning, as young as Nicole, she'd have an entire life for her family and friends to sift through.

"I know Hal and Nicole's parents would both appreciate having all her things from here, but you better hold off on that a little while longer." She looked puzzled and I knew I had to explain further. "Nicole's death is a police matter at least until there's some ruling on her death. Right now it could be suicide, an accident or even murder." Catalina's large blue eyes widened as I talked, and

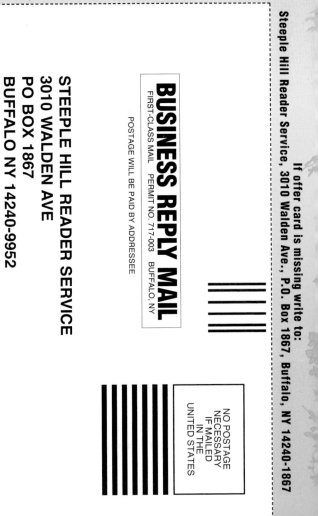

I could see that even as a nurse she hadn't thought of some of those possibilities.

"Murder? Who would want to kill somebody like Nicole? She wouldn't have ever hurt a fly."

"Neither would Hal, but until the county sheriff's department has their answers to how Nicole died and why, everybody around her may be under suspicion. And he'll be under the most suspicion..."

"Because he was the closest to her," Catalina finished. "I get that part. But I feel sorry for him. From everything Nicole said, he was great." She stopped, turning red. "Whoops. I guess I ought to watch what I say around you, huh? You being the ex and all."

"Trust me, I'm pretty much over Hal as far as romance is concerned. My worries are more for our son. He's not quite nineteen and I don't want to have him watch his father go through something like this if I can help it."

We'd wandered pretty far off track here and I needed to get back to the subject we started with. "But that's not the issue here, Nicole's stuff is. I'd leave her cubicle just like it is now until whoever the county sheriff's department sends comes to investigate. They'll want to see as much as possible of what it looked like before."

Catalina winced. "It's going to be hard to convince them that nobody's been through it all already, then. Nicole was kind of disorganized on the best of days. She was forever misplacing stuff. Like her car keys, for example. Her spare car key has been gone for about a month, I think. Because of the way she lost stuff and looked for it, her desk was pretty cluttered a lot of the time."

"That's funny. The house was nearly perfect." After I said that I thought a minute. "But that was probably Hal's influence, wasn't it?" The man had been a neat freak most of his life. He wouldn't have changed that just for Nicole. I wondered what kind of discussions they had about his little quirks and probably hers, as well.

"Yeah, Nicole always said he was trying to reform her." Cat gave a sad smile. "I don't think it was working, though. The only thing she really complained about was the way he wanted everything arranged at the house. I think she rebelled by keeping things here in a worse mess than she would have normally."

I tried not to laugh. With Nicole dead this was more moving than funny, but in any other set of circumstances I would have said it served Hal right. I didn't have time to respond, though, because of the commotion that started in the courtyard from someone bursting through the doors closest to the hall where Linnette always went for her therapy session.

"I told her about the agents! That's why they did that to her. Now they're going to be after me." Zoë stood, wild-eyed and shaking for a moment, then bolted across the courtyard. Her nimbus of brown hair looked more disordered than usual, and she wore a jacket she must have culled from somebody else, judging from the way it fit her. Wherever she'd gotten it, the original owner had taste and some money, because it was nicely cut and of good fabric.

"Hey, slow down there. Let's find somebody to talk to you." Catalina bounded up from the bench and crossed half the space between them to try to calm her down. "C'mon, Zoë. We can help you with this."

Zoë backed through the door at the far end of the courtyard. "No you can't. Nobody can. I can't trust anybody. Not even him." Before Catalina could reach her Zoë bolted out the doors that led through the lobby. It would only take a minute or two for her to be off the hospital property.

"Can you do anything?" I asked Catalina, who pulled out a walkie-talkie and spoke into it briefly.

After a moment she looked at me and sighed. "If she's off hospital grounds? Not really. She's not an inpatient, she wouldn't sign herself in voluntarily, and just being freaked out over Nicole's death isn't something that we can have her arrested or committed for. Unless she does something a lot worse, she's out there on her own."

Cat's brow wrinkled. I didn't know her well enough to know whether she was worried about Zoë or just thinking hard. I figured it couldn't hurt to ask. "What's wrong?"

"I wish I could have said the right thing to calm Zoë down and keep her here. She got out of here so quickly, I didn't get a chance to ask her something."

"Was it important?"

Cat nodded slowly. "I think she was wearing Nicole's jacket, and I wanted to ask her where she got it."

"Maybe you'll get another chance," I told her. Through the heavy glass doors into the front area I could see across the lobby to Ray Fernandez, leading a reluctant Zoë back into the building.

Twenty minutes went by before Ray got everything sorted out. Once he established that Zoë was an outpatient and not escaping somehow from the hospital, he let her go. "You might want to stay around here while I talk to people," he told her, more gently than I expected. Now his tone with me was another story. When he got done glaring he used about the same kind of voice Buck Morgan uses with a recalcitrant dog he's training.

My explanation that I was there to drive Linnette to her group therapy session didn't make him much happier. "What I saw was definitely not driving. So have a seat on that bench and we'll talk once I'm done asking a few questions of the staff."

Not wanting to intensify an argument, I sat. Soon Linnette and others came through the door, apparently done with their session.

Following them was another dark-haired young woman who looked about the same age as Nicole. I figured this was Monica, and tried to think of a way to verify that with Linnette without being loud enough to attract Ray's attention.

I motioned to the empty place beside me on the bench. When she got there I told her as quietly as possible what was going on. And I learned from her that yes, the young woman with dark hair and a slightly troubled expression was indeed Monica. There was a little time to talk, as we weren't the main focus of anybody's attention right now. Neither was Zoë.

The moment Zoë realized that nobody was going to force her to stay any longer she sidled to the door into the lobby and vanished. If Fernandez wanted to ask her any more questions right now he was out of luck. So was Cat.

I knew Ray would be upset with himself when he realized he'd let Zoë go. However, the man had said he didn't want to hear anything else from me, and he wasn't going to. Let him figure out himself that the woman he'd just released on her own recognizance was wearing a piece of clothing belonging to a murder victim.

"How much longer will he want to keep us here?" Linnette kept her voice as quiet as I had. She'd gotten a little experience watching Ray work a few times now and she knew how little interference he tolerated during his investigations.

"I'm not sure. He can't be too interested in why we're here but I'm afraid to leave without Ray giving us the okay."

"What were you doing out here while I had my session?"

I shrugged. "Talking to Cat. She actually approached me. In fact if he asks her what we talked about he'll know that I told her to do things exactly the way he would want them done. Not that I'll get any credit for that."

"Hey, it might happen." Linnette liked Ray enough she usually took his side on issues. She straightened up and I looked over to see him finish talking to Cat and head in our direction.

"Okay, why don't you two head on home? If you're truly here just to drive Ms. Parks to and from her session, you won't mind leaving now, right, Gracie Lee?" His golden-brown eyes showed more than a hint of challenge.

"Fine. I appreciate you being so understanding, Detective Fernandez." The look of surprise he gave us warmed my heart. Ray might have expected an argument from me on this issue, but he was right. If Nicole really had been killed by someone else and not just gone for a midnight dip after drinking too much, then the sheriff's department should come to that conclusion on its own. "By the way, did Catalina tell you what we were talking about?"

His answering grin was swift. "Why do you think I'm letting you go? For once you showed enough common sense not to get involved in a murder investigation and you gave somebody else good advice, as well. Now I'd like you to leave before the temptation to revert to your normal behavior becomes too great for you to resist."

Next to me Linnette stifled a tiny laugh. She covered beautifully, making it sound like a cough instead, but I recognized the true nature of her noises. And this woman called herself my best friend. "Perhaps we'll speak again soon, Detective." Without another word to either of them, I headed toward the lobby.

Linnette caught up with me before I cleared the doors to the outside world. "Hey, don't get grumpy. You have to admit he's got a sense of humor."

"Yeah, but it's harder to appreciate when it's directed at me," I admitted. "So was there anything else that happened back there that you could actually tell me about?"

"Not a whole lot. Monica seems very nice. Most of the participants in the group session were surprised to hear about Nicole. Zoë wandered in after everybody else got there. Did you see her cross the courtyard?"

"No, come to think of it, I didn't. And I think that even while I was talking to Cat we would have noticed her."

Linnette shrugged. "Security is supposed to be very tight here, but there must be ways around it because that's not the first time I've seen people slip into therapy sessions late, coming from somewhere other than the courtyard. Something about Zoë's appearance startled Monica anyway."

We got in the car while I filled her in. "Cat said she thought Zoë might be wearing one of Nicole's jackets. I'm not sure how that might have come about. Cat also told me that Nicole was always misplacing things, and that her spare set of car keys has been gone for a while."

"Were any keys found with the body?"

"Nothing much was found with the body besides underwear and a necklace. And I'm pretty sure that the investigators don't know where the body went into the water." I stopped talking to reverse the car out of its spot and get out of the lot. "I imagine there's some kind of formula they use to figure out where a body probably entered the ocean from where it's found."

Linnette sighed. "And you know that nobody's going to share that formula with us. You'd think that one of those TV shows about forensics would explain it all, anyway."

"They might, but with the number of things I've gotten wrong from listening to various cop shows and movies, I think I'll stick to the Science channel from now on." It might be boring, but at least a certain detective wouldn't laugh at me as much.

Driving down the freeway with the breeze whipping through my hair, I was surprised to realize how much Ray's regard of me mattered. *Better watch yourself,* I thought silently. Once a man's opinions started to matter, commitment was just around the corner. And at this point in life, it was a corner I couldn't afford to turn.

TEN

We all had plenty to talk about at Christian Friends that evening. Linnette insisted that I lead the group, with her walking me through everything. She explained why right after opening prayer and welcoming. Almost everyone knew she'd been depressed, but not all of them were aware of the extent of her problems this time around.

I was struck once again by what a good bunch of people I had for friends. Everyone gathered around Linnette, gave her empathy and asked how they could help. Paula hadn't made the meeting tonight, but I was sure that even she would have been supportive and caring. In the outside world some people treated those with emotional illness unkindly, but in here we were there for each other all the time. Maybe there was a situation that this group of praying women couldn't handle, but so far it hadn't come up.

"So, besides Gracie Lee driving you places when you needed somebody, let us know what you've been doing for yourself," Dot asked. Linnette's explanation of her battle over the last few weeks and the steps she and her doctor had used to treat it helped lead into my concerns over Hal. Once the group understood the connection between Nicole as Linnette's therapist and also as Hal's fiancée, they started asking questions about Nicole's death. The last time most of the people in this room had heard anything about her, we were lightly calling her a runaway bride. Now the situation was so much more serious and Hal might be in deep trouble.

Neither Linnette nor I could answer all their questions about what might have happened to Nicole over the weekend, but Lexy helped out by answering some of ours. "Now remember that I'm no expert in criminal law. I do entertainment law, contracts and agreements and negotiations. But I haven't forgotten everything I learned in law school."

"I hope not. It wasn't that long ago," Linnette told her. Lexy made a wry face.

"I'm glad somebody thinks so. In the legal world, five years can be forever if you don't keep up with stuff."

Lexy confirmed what I already feared; if the medical examiner ruled that Nicole's death was a homicide, Hal would be the most likely suspect. "The good thing is that there's no hard physical evidence that points toward him. Cases are made on circumstantial evidence alone, but they don't usually result in convictions. Most district attorneys want more, especially when there's not a celebrity angle."

"Do you think her father being a well-known plastic surgeon would give the case enough notoriety to put Hal in trouble?" Heather asked the question, citing one of those things we'd learned from the newspaper. It didn't mean that much to me, but then I wasn't a Californian, either. If Nicole's father had enough star-quality clients, the media could latch on to this.

"Better hope he's very good, but not working on a lot of well-known people," Lexy said, confirming my suspicions. "The fact that he's in Newport Beach means that he might draw less limelight. But we're all working under the assumption that the medical examiner will find evidence of foul play."

Dot made a noise that sounded like "harumph." It was out of character enough that we all looked at her. "Since when does the media around here wait for full facts? And judging from what I've seen in the paper already, *something* happened to that young woman. People don't accidentally ingest a heavy amount of alcohol and end up in the ocean unless they're having a party on a pier or a boat."

She had a point. While I felt real comfort from the way everyone had rallied around Linnette, I needed their help, as well. "Dot's probably right," I told them. "And even though you've heard me complain more than once about Hal as an ex-husband, and for the way he parents Ben, I can't imagine that he would murder anybody."

Lexy shook her head, making her blond shoulder-length hair bounce in heavy waves. "I hate to say it, Gracie Lee, but that's just what a good defense lawyer would say in court. And no matter who says it, a district attorney isn't going to listen."

We sat quietly sipping our coffee for a while, everyone trying to come up with something positive to say. In the end I changed the subject to Ben's engagement announcement. While the Christian Friends didn't have any words of wisdom for Hal's situation, they had plenty for Ben's. Again, it was Dot who had the best advice. "Make the two of them sit down and tally up the costs of marriage. Not a wedding, but the marriage that comes afterward. Once they see all those figures it might be a deterrent. And if it isn't, at least you'll know they're going into this with their eyes open."

It made good sense. I had a fairly good idea that

neither of these kids had a clue what the basics in life truly cost. A full day carrying around a notebook and jotting down the costs of everything might provide a rude awakening for my lovestruck son.

Ben sat at the breakfast bar, milk dribbling off his spoon and back into his cereal bowl when I told him about Dot's suggestion. "Are you serious about that?"

"Yes, I am. I thought it was a very good idea." Eight o'clock felt a little early to get defensive, but there it was. I needed coffee and while there was plenty of coffee in the apartment there weren't any coffee filters. Since I wasn't about to stoop to using a paper towel, coffee was going to wait until I made a store run.

"No, I'm not putting it down, Mom. I'm just really surprised that you're suggesting it. I thought you were just going to keep arguing against this. I wasn't expecting anything like acceptance." His grin almost made me cry. It felt so good to know that my opinion still mattered that much to him.

"This isn't total acceptance, but I'm working on it," I told him, giving him a hug from behind, over the chair. "I just want to make sure you two really, really understand what you're getting into."

"Hey, given the example you and Dad have set,

you ought to be glad I'm even thinking about marriage."

"I'd have to agree with you on that one, Ben. I just wish you'd think about it a year or two longer before committing yourself." Even behind him I could feel the eye roll Ben gave me.

An hour later in the grocery store I tried to juggle the coffee I'd bought at their coffee counter, put the coffee filters into my cart and pull my ringing cell phone out of my purse before it stopped ringing. The Caller ID flashed Hal's number. "Hi. How's it going?" The minute the words were out of my mouth I wanted to call them back. *It was going horribly...how else could it possibly be going?* "Ack. Forget I asked."

"No, that's all right. It's reflex, I understand. I won't even try to answer." There was a long pause and it felt as though Hal was trying to collect himself before he went on. "Look, could you come over? I need to talk to somebody who doesn't think I killed anybody, harmed anybody or made a gigantic fool of myself and, well, you're the only person I could think of."

I felt like telling him he could have tried his son, but I wasn't sure that Ben would agree, especially with that proviso about being a fool. By now I was so embedded in this whole mess it was difficult to see a way out. "Sure. Give me twenty minutes to finish up at the grocery store and I'll come over, okay?"

"Fine. Did you just say that you're at the grocery store?"

I could see where this was leading, so I didn't even resist. I tried to remember how much help I'd needed after Dennis died, and the way my Christian Friends group had given me all that help. Maybe I should just treat Hal as I would another group member in the same situation. "I sure am. And I haven't gone through the checkout line yet. What do you need?"

"Coffee filters. I have no idea where Nicole kept them. And get me a loaf of white bread and a dozen eggs. I mean real eggs and not that egg-whites-in-a-carton stuff."

"Will do. I'll be there soon with everything." Or at least a sack of groceries. I had an idea Hal needed much more than I could provide.

Half an hour later I sat at his kitchen table refreshing my coffee from the grocery store with the fresh stuff he'd brewed using his new coffee filters. At least he could make coffee once he had the filters. "So I'm pretty sure you didn't call me just to bring you groceries. What did you want to talk about?"

Hal put the coffee back on the warmer and sat down. "Everything. My entire life feels like a train wreck. My parents are at the mall because Mom didn't bring anything she could wear to a funeral instead of a wedding. My in-laws won't speak to me because they think I had something to do with their daughter's death. And…and I'm afraid they might be right."

Well, that made me nearly spit out my coffee. I steadied myself on the edge of his kitchen table and tried to be rational. "What do you mean? I think you'd know one way or another, wouldn't you?"

"Well, I didn't do anything to her, I mean physically. It's just that…we sort of had a…discussion before she went out with her friends."

"How serious a discussion? Like, an engagement-ending discussion?"

"I didn't want it to be. But Nicole started out by asking me what I thought about maybe delaying the wedding a little while. I didn't react well to the idea. We may have only been engaged since Christmas but we've been dating quite a while. And like my parents and hers are so fond of pointing out, I'm not getting any younger. She'd talked about kids and I didn't want to wait until I'd be playing touch football with a walker."

The whole picture in my mind was so unattractive that I just set down my coffee and stopped risking it going down the wrong pipe. "So you didn't discuss why she wanted to delay things, or for how long?"

He shook his head. "No. Things started getting tense after that. She said she just felt overwhelmed. I started ranting on how overwhelmed she'd feel if she told her mom she was canceling a wedding that was supposed to happen in two weeks. We yelled some, didn't settle anything and she stormed out."

"Do the police know this?"

"Not exactly." He took a drink of his own coffee and looked down at the surface of the table and cursed softly. "No, they don't know any of it. And now I'm afraid it will just make me look worse that I didn't tell them right away."

"Maybe so, but I think you still need to tell them. Knowing that Nicole was that upset when she went out with her friends might put a different light on things."

His brow furrowed. "I don't think she was upset enough to do anything foolish. Not on purpose, for sure. But she might not have made the best decisions during the evening."

"That's why you should tell someone at the sheriff's department."

Hal opened his mouth to say something and closed it again when the phone rang. Answering it, he didn't make any effort to hide his end of the conversation, which seemed to involve credit cards. A few minutes later he hung up and turned to me. "Something's happened and it's really weird. At least it's weird for me. The detective sounded like he hears it all the time."

I resisted asking him which detective he was talking to. I'd rather not know. So far I didn't have any real confirmation that Ray was the lead detective. "It sounded like you were talking about credit cards. What's up?"

"When they were here for me to report Nicole missing, the officer taking the information asked about her credit cards. I gave them a list of the three that I knew about, one joint account and two that were all hers. One of hers has had hits on it last night and today. The detective was calling to verify that I didn't have access to the account."

"And you don't, do you?"

Hal shook his head, looking very confused. "No, but somebody does and they're buying things at stores less than twenty miles from this house."

"Did the detective tell you what happens next?" As long as Hal could prove he wasn't using the card, maybe this meant he'd be less of a suspect in Nicole's death.

"Next they track down the person who's been using the card and try to figure out how they got it, or if they even have the actual card. Of course your detective Fernandez told me the same thing they said last time…not to go anywhere outside the county without notifying them."

My heart sank a little to know that Ray was in charge of this case. The last place I wanted to be was between these two men, especially when it involved an issue this serious. I prayed silently that this would resolve quickly. If I'd known then how quickly Ray would have an answer, and where that would lead, I would have been a little more specific with my prayers.

Once I left Hal's house I went home with the rest of my groceries and put everything away, mulling over all the while how I was going to make a phone call. Ben and I spoke briefly before he headed off to talk to one of the managers at the office supply store. He actually wore pressed khakis and a shirt with a collar, making me think he might get the job. "And while I'm there I'm going to buy a little notebook," he said, making a goofy face at me. "I'm going to give your suggestion a try for a couple days. Not that I expect I'll have any big surprises."

"Oh, yeah? Let me give you two words. Car insurance." He turned a little pale and lost the funny expression.

"Huh. I guess married people can't be on their mom's car insurance, can they?"

"Not exactly. Go online sometime after you get home from your interview and check rates. It won't be pretty."

He smiled weakly. "Great. Any other 'words' for me?"

"Not yet. Maybe I'll think of some later." He left before I came up with any more and once he was gone I started practicing my phone call out loud. Just about the time I'd worked my courage up my cell phone rang. It was Ray, giving me a momentary panic because I was all set to call him.

"Hi. We've got to talk," he said.

"Right. To say that we can't talk. Or get together, or anything else for a while. Correct?"

The noise he made on his end of the phone made me picture him slowly massaging a temple as if he had a migraine. "That would about cover it. I take it you've been talking to your ex again."

"Yes, and I'm likely to be talking to him at least once a day until things settle down and you decide he had nothing to do with Nicole's death. Or..." I couldn't force myself to talk about the other possibility.

"Or we decide that he did. In any case we can't see each other socially while this investigation goes on. Even if I handed it over to somebody else, which I can't right now, I'd feel uncomfortable with us going out right now."

"I understand. I was just about to call you and tell you the same thing. I don't want to get you in trouble or color your judgment in any way."

"I wouldn't worry about that part. I'm hard to sway," he said.

"I've noticed, but we won't get into that now."

He sighed. "Will we ever get into it now? Depending on how this ends, I can imagine you not wanting to see me again."

That sent pain through me in a couple ways, and I knew Ray wanted me to answer right away, but I couldn't. After a couple of deep, slow breaths I leaned against the wall. "If all you do here is do your job and do it honestly and well, I can't fault you if things don't turn out the way I want them to."

Now it was his turn to stay silent for a while. "We'll see what you say later, Gracie Lee. I'll call you when I can, and I promise that anything that I can tell you, I'll make sure you hear before you have to get information from the media or gossip."

"I appreciate that. Is there anything you can tell me now?"

"Not much. Only that if you saw that homeless woman slip out of Playa del Sol yesterday, I wish you would have told me. Maybe if I hadn't been so busy chewing you out for being there you would have been more cooperative, huh?"

"Maybe," I told him, surprised at how hard it was to see through the tears that gathered. "I'll miss you, Ray. Know that I'm praying for you."

"Usually I'd have a smart remark about that, but

today I'll just say thank you." We said a few more uncomfortable goodbyes and I put down the phone to grab a paper towel and wipe my eyes. Of all the times for Ray to get sweet on me. I sat there praying that when all this was over, he'd still be willing to talk about faith.

Then I got to thinking about what else he said. He didn't exactly come out and tell me that Zoë was involved with Nicole's missing credit card but it made sense. A couple of things I'd seen while sitting in that same courtyard where we'd argued yesterday made me want to call him back. How did I do that without breaching anybody's confidence? And was I really sure about what I'd seen? I left Ben a note, grabbed my car keys and went to find Linnette. She was the one person I could think of who might help me find the answers.

ELEVEN

Summer session at Pacific Oaks meant odd hours for Linnette in the bookstore and for everybody at the Coffee Corner, especially in that period of limbo when graduation was over but summer classes hadn't yet started. Linnette and the staff used the time to catch up, do inventory and restock. Maria kept the coffee shop open on short hours with limited staff for the faculty and college staff who worked no matter what time of year it was.

All that meant I had no trouble finding a quiet corner there to get a couple of lattes and sit down with Linnette when I convinced her to take a break and talk to me. She listened while I told her about my conversation with Ray and what he'd said and hadn't said about Zoë and Nicole's credit card. I recounted how we'd both agreed that we shouldn't talk while he continued to investigate Nicole's death.

"But of course the minute I hung up after talking to him I thought of something I should tell him."

"Wow. We both know how delighted he'd be if you called him back an hour or two after saying you shouldn't talk any more during the investigation." Linnette had seen enough of Ray during a couple of situations involving the Christian Friends that she didn't have to be told how he'd react. "So how important do you think this is?"

"It could be serious if I really saw what I think happened. Let me see if you can add to what I recollect. On either the second or third therapy session I drove you to, Nicole came in later than usual, with Zoë closely following after her."

"Right. I remember because Nicole seemed a lot more harried than usual. She came into our session apologizing for being late. Then a few minutes later when we were talking about our highs and lows since the last week, Zoë started to say something about where she'd spent the night before. Nicole led her off on a different subject very quickly."

"I know that what I'm about to suggest would mean that Nicole broke about half a dozen rules and regulations as a therapist, but do you think she might have taken Zoë home with her? She seemed as unhappy as any of us when she found out that Zoë had to leave Playa del Sol as quickly as she did."

Linnette didn't speak for a few moments, and I could see her mulling the possibilities over in her mind. "It's a real possibility. That would explain several things about that day. Zoë seemed a lot more put-together than usual, like somebody had been looking after her. And Nicole was even more disorganized and stressed than usual, as if she had something heavy on her mind."

"So how do I get Ray to consider this? Without any more facts than I have, he'll just dismiss this as 'women's intuition' and we know how much store the great detective sets in that."

Linnette made a wry face. "Yeah. None whatsoever, as he's been so clear in the past." She sipped her latte and thought for a while. "Since you can't call him, maybe I can call or go over to his office and tell him what I saw. It wouldn't be violating doctor-patient confidences because I'm the patient. As long as I don't get into what anybody else said of a personal nature in the therapy session, I don't think that's a problem. And I might be able to mention what my chauffeur could add without mentioning her name." She smiled at me.

"Thanks. I owe you one," I told her.

She waved me away with an open palm. "You've done so much for me recently, I'm just happy to be able to pay back a little."

"Friends don't keep score. Especially as part of a Christian Friends group as tight as ours."

She smiled again. "That's because God doesn't keep score, either, fortunately for all of us. Instead He gave us Somebody who's wiped our scoreboard clean."

On that note we stood up, gave each other a hug and got ready to go on with our day. "Call me when you know something," I called as Linnette headed back to the bookstore to do more inventory. She smiled and nodded, giving me a wave. Then I stayed awhile to help Maria take stock of all the paper goods before heading home myself.

Halfway home I got to thinking that I hadn't called my mom in over a week. I'd probably use all my remaining cell phone minutes for the month to catch her up on the last six days. When I pulled onto the driveway beside the apartment I stayed in the car and dialed her number. My stomach felt like it did the last time Ben talked me into riding the log flume at Six Flags. Telling Mom everything felt about like staring down that final descent. We exchanged hellos and she told me the latest about life in Missouri. Then she asked me how things were going out here. I took a deep breath and plunged in. "Well, Mom, remember when I was nineteen and you told me you hoped that someday I got a kid just like me? Well, guess what Ben came home and told me on Saturday…?" After that the whole story tumbled out.

Forty-five minutes later I went up the stairs to the apartment, humming to myself. Nothing took more weight off my chest than getting sympathy from my mother. I felt even lighter than when I'd walked out of our Christian Friends meeting last night. When she doesn't think I've done something incredibly stupid, Mom listens like nobody else. Since stupidity wasn't my problem in this case, I knew I'd sleep better tonight than any time in the last week.

Tidying up the apartment and grabbing Dixie for a walk afterward would guarantee a good night's sleep. I got the dog and took my cell phone on my walk in case Linnette called with any news, but it was after dinner that night before she got back to me.

"Do you think Lexy can help find Zoë a lawyer better than the public defender she'll get otherwise?" Linnette asked. "After what I overheard today, I know she's going to need it."

That didn't sound so good. "Tell me all about it."

She recounted her trip to the station, waiting for Ray in the waiting room we both knew too well. "He was interested in what I had to say. And I think he was grateful that you'd passed on information without calling him yourself. Before I could leave, an officer in uniform brought Zoë in."

"How did she look?"

"Better dressed than before, still wearing that green jacket, but really off kilter otherwise. She acted really agitated, speaking loudly and not making a lot of sense."

She paused for a minute and I could sense reluctance in her voice when she continued. "I don't think she is going to do Hal a lot of good, Gracie Lee. She kept insisting that it was okay that she had Nicole's stuff because the man had given it to her."

That sounded even worse. "Go on," I urged, even though I knew I'd hear things I didn't want to hear.

"She told Ray and anybody else who'd listen that the man had thrown her out of where she was staying. But before he did that, he gave her the jacket and Nicole's credit card and keys, and told her never to come back."

Even with Zoë's mental health history to take into account, Hal didn't look too good right now. This could all be a part of Zoë's delusions, but if it wasn't, my ex-husband had a lot of complicated explaining to do. For the first time my belief in his total innocence crumbled just a little. If he'd neglected to mention something this important there had to be a reason. I just couldn't think of any that made sense if he had nothing to do with his fiancée's death.

* * *

Friday morning came and with it my only paid shift at the Coffee Corner for the weekend. When I worked I turned off my cell phone and gave my undivided attention to the work, even as a barista. I figured I needed to get used to leaving my two worlds separate because in another six months or so I could be in a counseling job somewhere. Working for Pacific Oaks as a counselor would be fantastic and so would working for the community college where Heather worked. Still, I couldn't worry about that too much now. For now I'm a student and barista, both of which take a lot of time. Worry over a possible job after graduation just doesn't fit into the picture.

The reduced number of faculty, staff and students on campus meant a light load for the morning. We got a lot of things done that usually had to wait until the coffee shop closed. By the time I finished my shift at one, the equipment all shone inside and out and I'd learned a couple new tricks on the blenders that make all our frozen summer concoctions. I turned my cell phone back on while I walked to my car in the parking lot.

Four new messages popped up on my voice mail. I listened to them all before I started my drive home. Hal's voice came up twice, sounding more agitated the second time. Ben called once, letting me know he'd gotten one step closer to a summer job and was going to go to the store to fill out paperwork and get the forms to take to a lab for a drug test. That sounded strange to me at first, but I suspect that in this day and age a lot of places want their employees to take a drug test before they start work there. At least they appeared to be serious about offering him a job.

The last message left me unsure of how to react. Only a day before Ray Fernandez said we'd have no contact with each other. Now here was his voice on my phone. "Hi, Gracie Lee. I promised to keep you in the loop about everything important that I could. I've left word with Ms. Barnes's family that her remains will be released to the funeral director of their choice by tomorrow morning. And I had to call your ex to ask him to come in to the station. If he doesn't have one already, it's probably time for him to retain the services of a lawyer. Sorry. I'll talk to you later."

Anger that Hal was being questioned based on the word of a disturbed and possibly delusional individual warred with gratitude that Ray kept true to his word and told me everything. At least I now knew why Hal's messages sounded so stressed. Given his business dealings in the Los Angeles area he more than likely had legal contacts. I debated on whether to call him or to just drive to

Tuscany Hills. Pretty soon my car is going to know the way by itself.

Hal's kitchen got more familiar with every trip to his house. By now I could make coffee without asking questions. While he sat at the kitchen table and made phone calls, I did just that. Judging from his end of the conversations Ellie didn't seem to be on speaking terms with him any more. How much had she learned from the sheriff's department? With Ray in charge I couldn't imagine she had much official information.

About the time I put a steaming mug of coffee in front of him Hal finished his fourth or fifth call. "Well, I now have one thing I never thought I'd need…a criminal attorney. And if I can't convince Ellie Barnes otherwise, I'm going to have no part in planning Nicole's memorial service." He buried his head in his hands. "How on earth did things come to this?" His voice cracked.

What should I say? I didn't want to reveal more than I should about what Zoë told the sheriff's department, but then again she'd apparently told the whole sheriff's department most of it, along with anybody else on the lower level of the building last night. "You already said that you didn't tell the police everything about your argument with Nicole Friday night. Is there anything else you might not have shared with them?" I hated to use the same tone and kind of question I used to use with Ben when I wanted information, but if it worked so well with one Harris male, why not try on another?

When Hal looked up his eyes were red and he held back tears. "I can't tell them everything that happened on Friday and Saturday. If I do, Nicole's image with her co-workers and the doctoral program will be shot to pieces."

I took his hand across the table, making him look me in the face. "If you know something you're not telling, you've got two choices. You can damage a dead woman's reputation or you can probably be charged with her murder. Is protecting her worth it, Hal?"

He gave a shuddering sigh. "It should be. If she were still alive I wouldn't say anything. But I don't know what's right anymore in this situation, or even if the police will believe me if I tell them the truth."

"Would you like to pray about it? That's what I normally do with the biggest decisions in my life these days." Okay, so I stepped out on a limb here. We're supposed to be bold in our faith, right?

Hal surprised me. "I've got nothing to lose. Start me out, because I'm not sure I can do this out loud myself."

He grasped both of my hands with a grip I might have protested as being way too strong under any other circumstances. I closed my eyes to center myself in order to find the right words. What I said might not have been eloquent, but it led Hal to continue the prayer on his own. His words were heartfelt and fervent, and when he finished he pulled our still joined hands to his lips.

"Well, you could have waited until Nicole was cold, couldn't you?" At the acerbic words from his mother, standing in the doorway of the kitchen, Hal let go of my hands as if he'd been scalded.

My former mother-in-law hadn't changed much in the three years since I'd seen her last. She still colored her hair in the brunette shade that had probably been natural when Ben was a toddler. Her long, thin face wore the same expression of distaste seeing me always gave her. Hands on her hips, she glared at me with a look that could have ignited the kitchen matches next to the stove.

I pushed my chair back and stood up slowly. "Lillian, you've always known exactly the wrong thing to say to me, but this one takes the cake," I told her. Her outburst even left Hal just sitting there with his mouth open, unable to say anything. I looked down at him, ignoring the now-spluttering woman I wanted no part of. "Call me soon. We'll figure out your next step." And picking up my purse, I walked out and drove home. All the way home I prayed for God's peace for Hal, and the wisdom for him to do the right thing, both where Nicole was concerned and to avoid strangling his mother. The first would be far easier than the second.

Dealing with Lillian always makes me lose it, even when she's relatively benign. We never hit it off to begin with, and after she pushed Hal into baptizing our premature daughter and naming her after his sister, Emily, any desire I had to get along with her vanished. Our baby died as early in life as the aunt she'd been named for, and her death meant the death of our marriage. Lillian blamed me for Hal never pursuing the career she wanted for him in medicine and I blamed her for pushing our divorce.

In retrospect I probably shouldn't give her all the credit for that divorce, but then she ought to admit by now that her son bypassed medical school because he didn't have the ambition to be a doctor the way his mother wanted him to. He did just fine in his undergrad in psychology, and he'd used it with great skill to help build the home security business with his father.

In my growth as a Christian so far I've been able to make peace with a lot of people and by God's grace I can forgive most of them. I know someday I'll get to that point with Lillian, at least I hope so. I'm pretty sure it's what God would have me do, but so far she's my biggest stumbling block. And incidents like the one in Hal's kitchen didn't help any.

Once I got home I turned off my cell phone, resolved to let the machine pick up the apartment phone, perhaps for the whole weekend, and went to the Morgans' house to either vent to my friend and landlady Dot or to borrow a dog for a long, vigorous walk.

I'd lost track of time, forgetting that Dot and Buck take Dixie and Hondo out as therapy dogs virtually every Friday afternoon. So I ended up walking by myself, still briskly and for a long while, and talked to God while I walked. This time I made sure all my talking was silent, because I couldn't get Zoë and the way people looked at her out of my mind.

When I returned, feeling much calmer and very tired, the apartment phone ringing made me go to look at the Caller ID. Since the display showed Ben's cell phone I answered. "I got the job," he crowed. "How about we celebrate by having me bring home pizza?"

"Sure. Will that be pizza for two or three?"

"Let's make it three. I'll pick up Cai Li on the way home."

"Great. And I'll make a salad to go along with the pizza." In the six days since their big decision

I hadn't had any real time with both of the kids together. They were serious about getting married, and I probably needed all the practice I could get at being somebody's mother-in-law. After my set-to with Lillian today I wanted to make sure to try my best to avoid that kind of relationship with Cai Li. Nobody deserves as much strife as Lillian and I created with each other.

The three of us spent the evening celebrating Ben's new status as an employed person with pizza, salad, soda and a couple rounds of board games that gave us all the giggles. I spent as little time as possible thinking about Hal or talking about him. I told Ben the latest things we knew for certain about Zoë's statement to the sheriff's department. I shared my concerns about his father without telling Ben anything confidential about Hal and Nicole, and mentioned as little as possible about Lillian. While Ben's relationship with his grandmother wasn't the best, it was light-years better than mine and I saw no reason to possibly poison that.

Ben in turn shared the details of his training so far, what he'd be going through on Saturday and showed us the yellow shirt with his new company logo that he'd be wearing on the job. "So does being hired mean you'll have to shave?" I asked hopefully.

He smiled sweetly and patted my shoulder.

"Sorry, Mom. You're out of luck on that one. I can keep the beard as long as it's neat. I may need a bit of a haircut, though, because I need to keep the sides above my ears and the back off my collar."

"Rats. I might as well learn to like that goatee, because it looks like it's here for a while." I tried not to look too disappointed. I could think of half a dozen things that might be worth arguing about—facial hair wasn't one of them.

True to my resolve, I avoided answering the phones the rest of the evening and all of Saturday morning. I felt a brief pang of guilt for telling Hal to call me, then not answering the phone, but I still wasn't ready to deal with his problems again. Scattering sticky notes on every relevant page of the stack of books I'd checked out of the library for my final project kept me busy until about noon. By then my grumbling stomach had started to tell me I needed to take a break for lunch.

A knock on the door got me up from my chair just after I'd started to do a mental inventory of the fridge. I looked out the window to see who my visitor might be, and decided to open the door anyway.

"This not-seeing-each-other thing just isn't working out, is it?" Ray asked. Even though I knew he wasn't here just to visit, he looked so good. "I can't fault you for not keeping your end of the bargain, because you haven't answered either of your phones for at least twenty-four hours."

"This is true. You weren't the main reason for my not communicating, but I saw it as a bonus this time. For a change I followed your instructions to the letter."

He shook his head, apparently not sure whether to wince or grin. "How about I take you out to lunch somewhere nice and public and ask you a bunch of questions while we eat?"

"Sounds terribly romantic." At that he grimaced. "Let me get my keys and leave a note for Ben and I'll be ready to go."

TWELVE

Ray drove and we went to Mi Familia, a family-owned Mexican grill near my place that makes awesome fish tacos. Ray's been a regular there much longer than I have, and he still has to argue once in a while to be able to pay for his food. The owners would like to give it to him, but I'm glad he stays on the level and pays every time.

This time I even let him buy mine, because he told me this would be a business lunch. In a few minutes we sat at a corner table with a couple of tacos apiece and Ray's familiar notebook and pen on the table. He tells me a lot of people have switched to electronic devices for their notes and such, but I don't think he trusts them. We ate in silence for a while, with him looking over his notes. His cramped handwriting didn't lend itself to being read upside down, so I gave up and just ate my fish tacos.

Ray finished one of his tacos, wiped his mouth with a napkin even though I could have told him he looked fine, and looked at his notes one last time. "Okay, do you mind if I start asking you a few things while you eat?"

"Go ahead. I'll try to be polite."

"Have you mentioned anything about Nicole's missing keys to anybody?"

"One person. I told Linnette about it right after Catalina mentioned it to me. According to Cat, Nicole misplaced a lot of things. But then you probably know that already."

He didn't confirm or deny that, just went on watching me and asking questions. "So Linnette is the only person you even mentioned that to? You didn't tell Ben, or his father?"

"No. I can't think of any reason Ben would need to know that. I've said as little about Nicole as possible to him besides what's been in the paper or what's basically common knowledge. And I expected Hal to mention it to me if he knew about it, which I doubt he did."

Ray leaned forward. "What makes you say that?"

"Cat implied that Nicole kept her bad habits at work. Hal's always been kind of a clean freak with a high need for organization. He's the kind of guy who alphabetizes his CDs."

"Hey, what's wrong with that?"

I felt the urge to bury my head in my hands. "Don't tell me you do that, too?"

He looked away from me for a moment. "I might."

"Hmm. Maybe that part isn't so strange, after all. But unless other things have changed a great deal, Hal wouldn't react well to hearing that Nicole misplaced something as important as a set of car keys. Especially when I suspect he bought her the car fairly recently."

Ray looked thoughtful. "So it might not be surprising that he's the only one close to her who hasn't mentioned the car keys?"

"Not if the others you've talked to are her friends at work and perhaps her family."

He wrote something in his notebook and didn't say anything else for a while, letting both of us concentrate on lunch for a short time. Once he finished about half his taco he looked at me again. Ray seemed fidgety or uncomfortable, which made me wonder what kind of question would come next.

He couldn't quite meet my gaze all the way. "You've said Mr. Harris could be quite disapproving at times. Did he ever go past that to abuse, either verbal or physical?"

I put down my food, suddenly not very hungry anymore. "I can understand why you have to ask something like that. It's part of your investigation, and I am his ex-wife. But it still hurts a little to have to talk about it with you. No, Hal never harmed me. I only wish I could say the same about his mother."

I'd never seen a look on Ray's face quite like the one my statement prompted. "I'll put my notebook down so that this is totally off the record, but I want to hear more about that, Gracie." True to his word, he closed the notebook and put down his pen. Then he took my hand in his and focused those warm golden-brown eyes on me. Well, that made the floodgates open up for sure. More than sixteen years of hurt came pouring out while Ray listened.

By the time I'd finished I'd used at least two napkins to wipe tears away and Ray still held my hand. He may not have gotten all the information he wanted, but he'd certainly earned points with me in the relationship arena. "Aren't you sorry you asked?" I said, my voice still a little choked up and my throat a bit scratchy from talking and crying.

"Not at all. Hearing all of that taught me a good deal about three different people, and I think you all will matter quite a bit in the course of this investigation."

"What could Lillian possibly have to do with it all? When Nicole died, Hal's mom was in Tennessee and probably has a couple hundred witnesses to that, seeing as she must have been in the airport in Nashville instead of a beach in California."

"I know that it's not possible that either of Mr. Harris's parents actually killed Nicole Barnes. But they raised him and provided the behavior he would think of as normal. Looking at a person's family is often the key to understanding their actions and knowing what they're capable of."

His words made me wonder if Ray thought that Hal might be capable of murder, given his upbringing. Even as mean-mouthed as his mother is, I couldn't imagine he'd inherited anything from her but the ability to use sarcasm to wound those around him. I didn't want to ask Ray anything more because I would rather not put any more ideas in his astute head. Now that I'd finished crying I felt terribly aware of how I must look. I wanted to hide for a few minutes with a comb, mirror and lipstick.

I excused myself to go repair the damage. With what my purse held, I could do a little to better my appearance, anyway. Somehow I didn't think Ray would miss me nearly as much after this lunch. When I said something to that effect as we left the restaurant he put an arm around me. "I know, PDA is the kind we should be avoiding, but I can't help myself." His arm around me felt so good I had to fight leaning into it. "I'm beginning to think you're going to be a necessary information conduit for me in this case. And I'll miss you just as much this afternoon as I did this morning."

He put me in his car and drove me home, both of us saying little. I don't know about Ray, but I spent the time thinking a lot and trying to figure out just how things changed between us during lunch. He parked in the driveway next to my apartment before I realized we had arrived. "I think kissing you goodbye would be a very bad idea right now," he said, voice husky.

"I'm afraid you're right. For now we need to keep things a little bit more detached, at least until this case is over one way or another."

He looked at me more intensely, quirking one eyebrow. "What's up? That's the first time I've heard you say something besides strongly declaring Mr. Harris's innocence."

"I still think he didn't kill Nicole. But I'm also pretty sure that there are things he's not telling you, or even me that have bearing on the case."

"Now you're beginning to sound like me. That's a little scary, Gracie." I got out of the car before I had to admit what I found even scarier; I really wanted Ray to stay and discuss all kinds of things that didn't have anything to do with this case, or maybe discuss absolutely nothing for a while instead.

When I'd gotten halfway up the stairs he rolled down his car window. "Call me if you want to. And I'll call you once your ex has come in for his interview Monday morning, if I know anything I can share."

"Please do. Have a good weekend."

"I'll try." He waved and the window slid most of the way up, and then Ray was gone. Since Ben's car was still gone, I expected the empty apartment that greeted me. Now felt like a good time to get back in touch with the rest of the world, so I turned on my cell phone and went to see whose messages I'd missed on the answering machine.

Between the two phones there were several hang-ups or sales pitches, four calls from Ray and three from Hal. Ray's messages mostly said little; just that he had a few questions I could help him answer. The only different piece of news he gave me was that Zoë would remain in police custody for a while, charged for now with credit card fraud and theft. Hal's messages got more involved with each one, starting with apologies for his mother's behavior. On the last message he used as much time as the machine let him have.

"My parents are in their rental car driving up the coast to the Hearst Castle. They weren't helping anything here, and even I needed a breather from my mother. I shudder to think what she might say at Nicole's funeral. It looks like I'll be allowed to go to that event as long as I don't get arrested between now and Tuesday. And Ellie is threatening to come to the house and remove all of her daughter's belongings. Needless to say I have a locksmith coming to change all the locks." I could hear him sigh on the message. "Given Nicole's propensity for losing stuff, there's no telling how many keys to this house are floating around Ventura County."

That gave me pause. So Hal knew about at least some of Nicole's problems "mislaying" things. He didn't sound happy about it, and I would still guess that he didn't know about the car keys.

He asked me to call him when I could and hung up. That message had been left only half an hour before, while Ray and I ate fish tacos. I debated about when to call Hal back. I could only think of so much I could say to help him at this point and after the discussion at lunch I felt drained. The longer I stayed in the living room the more the couch called to me. A short nap couldn't hurt, I told myself. A short nap probably wouldn't have hurt, but the two hours I ended up dozing in an odd position left my neck stiff and my back complaining. At least when I woke up my emotional pain was far less than it had been earlier in the day.

After I made fresh coffee and drank a cup, I did something I'd never done before. I called Ben's cell phone and asked him to relay a message to his father for me. "Tell him that I'll call him after church tomorrow. Make sure he knows that I'm not abandoning him, I just need a little more time on my own." In all the time I'd been a single parent I'd been careful never to put Ben in the middle of any situations with his father and me. This time I hoped they'd both understand.

In the morning I went to church, and even made the extra effort to go to Bible class instead of hanging out with my friends for coffee. I saw a few of them anyway because Dot and Linnette both attended the same Bible class I chose. Afterward we stood in one of the broad hallways at Conejo Chapel, out of the way of the worst traffic but still together. I filled them in on as much as I could, with both of them listening attentively. "So Zoë's in jail at least temporarily, but you don't think Hal gave her the things she claims he did?" Linnette summarized.

"I don't think he did on purpose, anyway. I can't explain more than that because I'm not positive." Saying it that way sounded more vague than it should have been, but it was the truth. "I need to talk to Hal again, and I'd like to find out more about Zoë."

Dot nodded. "It sounds like she's the key here, unless she's just totally wrong about where the things she had came from."

"That's still a possibility. She's not a well individual." I'd seen enough just from her trips through the courtyard to know that Zoë had some serious problems.

Linnette leaned against the wall, looking thoughtful. "It's true that she definitely has some challenges, but at least three-quarters of the time when I've been with her, Zoë's version of what goes on around her is pretty much on track. Now when it's not, it's really not. But what she's said sounds like the truth as she knows it."

I'd been afraid of that. Part of me wanted to side with Dot's hope that Zoë had gotten Nicole's things a totally different way, some way that didn't implicate Hal in his fiancée's death. He'd told me he had a good criminal lawyer, didn't he? Surely he or she would give Hal far better advice than I ever could. Still, I promised I'd call him, and once I got home, I would.

"This is really taking a toll on you, isn't it?" Linnette laid a hand on my shoulder. She wore a worried look that made me want to reassure her. She was right, though, and I admitted that to her.

"I think for your sake, and maybe for mine as one of her few friends, we ought to check out Zoë's story as much as we can. Do you think Detective Fernandez would find anything illegal in our doing that?" Linnette's expression had changed from worried to merely thoughtful.

"I think we'd have to be very careful only to ask the kinds of questions a concerned citizen would ask about an acquaintance, and not cross the line into police territory."

Linnette brightened. "Well, I am concerned about her. As part of my assigned goals for these group therapy sessions I'm supposed to get back into normal routines and exhibit healthy concern for others. Zoë's as good as anybody else for me to exhibit healthy concern about."

"I don't know what bothers me more...the fact that I understand what you just said, or that I'm as eager as you are to do it." Linnette and I started laughing, while Dot just looked on. The look on her face said that she might think we both needed a little more group therapy.

Before Linnette and I set out to try to find Zoë's friends or family, I finally made the call I'd promised to make. Hal sounded as depressed as I'd ever heard him. When I tried to apologize, he cut me off quickly. "Look, I understand, Gracie Lee. You've probably had your fill of this whole situation, and Mom's comments were just the icing on the cake."

"No, I'm not giving up on you. I'll admit that my reaction to your mom was immature at best. She brings out the worst in me." I wasn't telling Hal anything new with that admission.

He gave a mirthless laugh. "She has that effect

on a lot of people. I can't tell you what your support means to me. I've thought a lot about what we prayed about Friday. And when I go into the sheriff's station tomorrow I'm going to tell Detective Fernandez everything. It's not like he's going to use this information to malign Nicole, only to find the truth in what happened to her."

"Amen to that. And hopefully finding the truth about what happened to her means that you will have a lot more peace in your life. I'll keep praying for that."

"Thanks. I appreciate it." We said goodbye and I changed out of my church clothes. Something told me that my nice skirt and blouse wouldn't win many friends in the places that Zoë and her friends spent their time.

I picked Linnette up at her house and she talked while I drove. "I called Monica, who I guess is my therapist now, and explained my interest in caring for Zoë if I could. She turned me over to one of the nurses, Catalina."

"Right. I've met her, remember?"

"I do now. Anyway, Catalina said that due to privacy laws she couldn't say anything particularly about Zoë. But she did say that many people with mental health problems live in one of the single-room hotels not too far from Playa del Sol that are filled with folks who are down on their luck."

"That has to be a hard existence."

"And that's the easiest it ever gets for Zoë. Catalina then said that many of their homeless or nearly homeless patients often live together at Camp Freedom."

The name rang a bell, but I couldn't think of why and I told Linnette so. "We've talked about it at church, as a possible outreach location. It's a place near the beach where the county is allowing a homeless encampment as long as things stay quiet. And that is our first stop."

THIRTEEN

Camp Freedom wasn't exactly what I expected. The county, on a contingency basis, had set aside a part of a large seaside park for the use of area homeless. There appeared to be about thirty people, many of them men who were probably Vietnam veterans. But while they might have been the majority, there were families and younger men and women on their own, as well. Several tents in good repair formed part of the encampment and even two "fifth-wheel" campers, both of which had seen better days, sat in among the tents.

I mentally chided myself for expecting more chaos when what I found was organization instead. People appeared to be working together, some cooking in one of the park fire pits with cast-iron skillets and pans while one young woman watched several children play on a swing set and three men sitting on old lawn chairs had a fairly loud discussion about something.

What surprised me most was that nobody looked or sounded scary or threatening, even the guys having their differences with each other. I felt embarrassed by my preconceived notions about what an encampment of homeless people, many of them mentally ill, might look like.

Linnette stood beside me as we took it all in. "Wow. Without medical insurance and an understanding boss, I could be in one of those tents," she said soberly. "I think that's why Zoë's problems disturb me."

"Hey, there are a few more differences between you and Zoë than a little money and a decent job," I argued. "You've got a supportive family and some good friends. You have an education and resources you can fall back on."

Linnette looked at me, eyes a little misty. "Don't you suppose Zoë might have had those things at one time? Depending on when she started showing signs of schizophrenia, she could have finished high school if not college, and lived the same kind of life you and I have for quite a while."

"You've thought about this a fair amount, haven't you?" I could picture Linnette lying awake at night, worrying about things like this. It made me want to hug her. Now probably wasn't the time, since we needed to start looking for someone who might know Zoë.

It didn't take long, by asking a few questions to the people who looked the most receptive, for someone to direct us to Joshua. If Camp Freedom had a mayor, it would be Joshua. I wasn't about to ask what the last name of the imposing man barbecuing hot dogs was, because everyone there called him by the one name. I had to admit that he looked a lot like an Old Testament prophet, other than the fact that this man wore a ragged UCLA sweatshirt and brown plaid pants.

Linnette took the lead as we approached him. "You Salvation Army?" he asked, eyeing us suspiciously. "If you are, you can clear out now. Everybody here is happy living here and they've got their reasons not to go to a shelter."

"No, we're not from Salvation Army or any other group like that. We're looking for people who might know Zoë McNamara." As Linnette spoke it dawned on me that this was the first time I'd ever heard Zoë's full name.

Joshua still looked at us as though we might steal his barbecue. "I might know her. Then again I might not. What do you want from her?"

"Nothing. I'm in her group therapy sessions at Playa del Sol and I know she's been arrested. I'm trying to find out where she spent a couple of nights last week."

His dark eyes narrowed to slits below his bushy gray eyebrows. "You a cop, then?"

"No, just another outpatient at Playa del Sol. I'll show you my ID if you like."

Linnette found her driver's license and showed it to him. He held it in one work-worn hand, eyes moving back and forth between the card and Linnette's face. "Okay. Thanks." He handed it back to her. "So why are you asking about Zoë?"

"Because she's involved in a murder investigation and her story may be the thing that either frees or convicts somebody."

He went back to grilling for a minute, turning the hot dogs before they burned. "I have to think it's somebody you two care about. Otherwise you wouldn't be down here talking to the likes of us."

"I might argue with that. Talking to you already makes me want to come back when I've got more time."

"Me, too." Both of them looked at me as if surprised I could speak. Seeing the encampment and talking to Joshua gave me a whole different perspective on Zoë. "But I want to ask something now, too. Did Zoë fit in here? Did she have somebody who looked out for her?"

"She fit in as well as anybody else. Better when

she took her meds, worse when she didn't." Joshua went back to his grilling, then turned and called to one of the women. "These are about done. Anybody got a plate?"

She nodded and ducked into one of the fifth-wheel campers. Walking briskly over to us, the young woman handed Joshua a blue-and-white plate that looked like the "unbreakable" dishes Ben and I used after the divorce until he got old enough that I could buy something a little more delicate. "Sunshine here could tell you as much about Zoë as anybody." She ducked back a little when Joshua mentioned her name. "It's okay. They're not cops or from a shelter or anything. You can talk to them."

She still held back a little, like a dog who's been kicked enough to be wary of everyone. "I'm in therapy with Zoë at Playa del Sol," Linnette said softly. That made Sunshine step a little closer, as if Linnette said the magic password. "Could we sit over there and talk a little?" She indicated the three lawn chairs that for the present were empty.

"Sure. But if Arnie and Gus come back, we've gotta give them back their chairs."

"Definitely," Linnette agreed. Then we sat down together and drew closer than the men had arranged the chairs. For a few minutes Linnette just talked about Zoë, how they'd gone to group therapy together, how she usually acted and what Zoë wore once she'd left the hospital. All the time Sunshine's long, slender fingers picked at her jeans, searching for loose threads and worn spots in the weave while she watched Linnette's face. "Last week Zoë was different. She seemed calmer and she followed our therapist around. Would you know anything about that?"

Sunshine stopped making eye contact. "She came back from the hospital and she was pretty healthy, for her. Zoë hears a lot of voices when she doesn't take her meds. But when she goes in, like she says, for a 'tune-up,' she stops talking about the agents for a while. She spent one night here, in my tent, after she got out. Then the next day me and her were up on Main Street, trying to get some spare change for…food and this lady came up to her."

"What did she look like?"

"Young. Real skinny. She had dark, shiny hair and didn't look happy. She told Zoë that she shouldn't be out on the street like that. Zoë told her she didn't have no place else to go. The lady looked real worried, and she looked all around, kinda like Zoë does when she's hearing the agents. Then the lady said Zoë should come with her. It was the last I saw of her for three or four days."

"Was she all right when she came back?" Linnette kept her gaze focused on Sunshine's face.

The girl, who looked much younger than Nicole, lifted one shoulder in a partial shrug. "I guess so. She wasn't hearing the voices yet. And she was dressed real nice. I think the lady must have given her stuff of hers, cause everything matched and it was pretty clean. Zoë even had a brand-new jacket."

"Did she say anything about that?"

Sunshine looked down at the patchy grass between our feet. "Only that somebody gave it to her. And it had stuff in the pockets. That night she bought us both dinner from the 7-Eleven with the change she had. After that she didn't go looking for loose change with me on Main Street no more. One day she brought me a sweater. Do you think I can keep it?"

Her green eyes were large and worried-looking. "For now, anyway," Linnette told her gently. "When was the last time you saw her?"

"A couple days ago. Thursday, maybe? When she got up that morning, she said she was going shopping. I asked her with what, and she said never mind. Then Gus said he saw her later and the cops were dragging her out of some store. I guess she got arrested."

"Yes, she did. The police say she was using somebody else's credit card."

Sunshine sighed deeply. "Oh, boy. If Zoë stays

in jail, the agents will come back pretty quick. It's going to be hard for her. Hard for anybody around her, too." We sat in silence for a moment after that, all picturing the kind of time Zoë McNamara would have in the Ventura County jail.

Back home that evening I got out a lawn chair of my own and sat outside for a long time, watching the sun set and the stars come out. I thought about Sunshine, who probably did that every night, but then went to sleep in a tent. Before we'd left, I'd asked her a little about her life and she'd showed us around. The county's agreement let the people from Camp Freedom use the beach showers nearby, a plus for most of the folks there.

It hurt my heart a little to realize just how good I had it, even when a few days ago I would have said I felt pretty low on the food chain. Compared to Hal's mini-mansion this apartment didn't look like much. When I thought about how the thirty or so people at Camp Freedom lived and considered themselves lucky, my life looked totally different. I thought about calling Hal, but again I didn't have much to tell him.

I had a pretty good idea by now what he wasn't telling the police. And I could figure out from there how Zoë actually had got that credit card and keys, and why she'd told Ray what she did. But Hal needed to clear that all up with the sheriff's department before I got involved. Perhaps after their meeting tomorrow I could breathe easier around either of these men.

Monday morning's paper mentioned Nicole twice. On the front of the local section there was an article about her body being identified, and the latest the medical examiner's office had released. Most of what that article said I already knew from one source or another.

It gave a few more family details in a different way than the obituary on page five. The news article said her father, Paul Barnes, was a "prominent Orange County plastic surgeon" and called Ellie a well-known fund-raiser for several charities. Meanwhile the family must have relented just a little in their decision to shut Hal out, because he was listed in the survivor's section along with her parents and sister. Sadly, two of her grandparents had outlived Nicole. I could only imagine the pain they felt.

With the rest of the family living more than fifty miles away, I'd wondered where any services would be held. There again the family must have let Hal have some little say in things because instead of being far away, tonight's gathering and tomorrow's services would be held just over the county line in Agoura, near Hal and Nicole's new home. With things located that close, Nicole's co-workers at

Playa del Sol and perhaps even some of her patients could possibly attend. After all my involvement in this, I would be attending, as well, and if Ray didn't like that he would have to live with it.

Ben worked six hours on Monday, starting fairly early. "I'll be home in time to pick up Cai Li, get dressed and go tonight. We'll meet you there," he told me before heading out the door. I hoped Hal realized what a good kid he had. Even though Ben didn't get along with Nicole's family very well, he decided even without being asked that it was important to be there for his dad. I felt proud of him anyway and intended to tell him so the first chance I got.

I paid more attention to the way I was dressed for Monday evening than I might have at another similar event. I wanted to be present, but not call attention to myself in any way. Like Ben, I'd be there to support Hal, but in a quieter way. When I talked to Linnette her decision not to come didn't surprise me any. She'd only had a few therapy sessions with Nicole, and I don't think she was up to going to a funeral home yet anyway. Just finishing the day at work still wore her out, and she'd already spent her day off talking to people at Camp Freedom. I felt relieved that tonight she'd stay home and get some rest.

Driving to Agoura didn't take very long, which

surprised me on a weeknight at six-thirty. Rush hour stretched to cover quite a bit of time here, though, and apparently most folks had headed home already on this Monday.

I had to get directions off the computer to find the place, yet another branch of Dodd and Sons. They seem to have the lock on the funeral and memorial business around here. It's just another industry where small local operations are slowly being taken over by larger national corporate entities. Buck Morgan often fumes that soon we'll get to the point where no matter what the service or product, we'll only have two choices. I'd argue with him but on a lot of things I'm not so sure he's off the mark.

The computer directions got me where I needed to go in one try—a rarity for me. Even after several years in the area there are a lot of places where I'm still learning the landscape. Each particular branch of the Dodd and Sons chain had its own different design. The one in Rancho Conejo had a 1950's A-line look reminiscent of a ski lodge, while the one in Simi Valley appeared to have been modeled after a California mission. This one looked less like a religious institution of any kind than the others, sporting a lot of glass, steel and concrete in spare lines.

Inside, the sparse, modern theme continued. A

sign outside what seemed to be the biggest of the three rooms available directed people to Nicole's visitation. The front of the room had floral arrangements so numerous I wondered if her family had taken the money already paid to the wedding florist and used it here.

Exotic orchids, bird-of-paradise flowers and unusual lilies sprouted from bouquets and pots. I debated about signing the guest book at the door, and then quickly scribbled my name with the "Harris" part a bit illegible. The Barnes family probably didn't want any reminders of Hal's former life.

Hal stood at one side of the front of the room, dressed in a dark suit, white shirt and somber tie. The fact that he was here and looked less stressed than I'd expected comforted me a little because it meant he hadn't been held by the sheriff's department. He stood alone, looking across a good twenty feet of space to where Nicole's family sat clustered together.

Ellie and Paige sat close to each other on folding chairs, the navy-blue of their outfits accenting the paleness of their skin and hair. The much larger man I assumed had to be Paul Barnes reminded me of the ravens I saw all over Rancho Conejo when I went for walks. His broad shoulders sloped in a perfectly fitted charcoal suit.

Silver trimmed the temples of his dark hair, cut short and styled neatly as I expected from a surgeon. He looked like he would be much more comfortable in scrubs under bright lights than he was here, draped in dark clothing and sitting, staring at his idle hands.

Sometime while I observed Nicole's family, Hal caught sight of me and indicated with a subtle movement that he wanted me to come closer to him. "Hey. I see the police didn't keep you," I said, cutting right to the chase. Hal wouldn't expect me to do anything else.

"Yeah, I took your advice. I told the detective exactly what was going on Saturday, and how I think that crazy woman got Nicole's keys and credit card."

I winced a little at him calling Zoë "that crazy woman" but then Hal has never been real politically correct about some things. I could only imagine some of the discussions he and Nicole had about her work. "Nicole brought Zoë home with her, didn't she?"

Hal looked down at the gray-flecked industrial carpeting and sighed. "She sure did. How did you figure that out?"

"I'm sure Nicole told you I'd been at Playa del Sol a couple times. I had a friend who needed transportation back and forth to one of Nicole's group therapy sessions. Zoë was part of the same group and I knew that everyone seemed concerned that she'd been more or less left on her own."

"Right, but no one else almost wrecked their reputation by putting a paranoid schizophrenic in their guesthouse." Hal fumed. "That was what half our argument the night Nicole disappeared was all about. She thought that if I couldn't understand why she did it and back her up, then maybe she should delay the wedding. I told her no matter how long she delayed the wedding, I still wasn't going to be happy with what she'd done."

"So what did you do Saturday morning when she didn't show up?" I asked, fairly sure I knew the answer to that question, too.

"I tossed her patient out as fast as possible. We needed the guesthouse for Nicole's family, and besides, I didn't want...Whatshername on the property any longer than necessary. She threw a fit, naturally, and I helped her gather up her stuff and get out of there. She asked if she could take the jacket and I said sure. I figured that if it had been out in the guesthouse it couldn't be anything Nicole cared much about."

"Bad choice, huh?"

"No kidding. I'd forgotten that Nicole had gone out there to work on her doctoral thesis rough draft a couple weeks ago. That memory lapse nearly got me arrested."

"I'm glad everything worked out okay."

Hal smiled weakly. "Yeah, me, too. It was good to tell my folks this morning when they got back from San Simeon that I was no longer the number one suspect in a murder. And I have you to thank for that." He took me by surprise by pulling me into his arms for a hug. I hugged him back, knowing he needed it but hoping that Nicole's family was otherwise engaged and not paying attention to us.

Hal stepped back from me suddenly, making me struggle a little for balance for a moment. "Whoops. I hope I didn't just get you in trouble."

At first I started to ask how he could possibly get me in trouble instead of things being the other way around. Then I turned and looked behind me to see Ray standing in the back of the room, frowning. From this distance I couldn't make out the vein in his temple but the rest of his expression told me that he probably had a migraine coming on.

FOURTEEN

I walked to the back of the room, unsure whether I should talk to Ray in this public forum or not. I decided to let him take the lead and he did. "Am I interrupting something?" he asked with ice in his voice. "I figured I'd see you here, but not quite that *close* to your ex. If he thought he was in deep trouble with Ms. Barnes's family before, he should catch her mother's look at him now."

"I think he's given up hope of getting back in their good graces," I told Ray. "Besides, that was just a friendly 'thank you' from Hal to begin with."

"Great. I wish I'd seen how you were going to say 'you're welcome.'" The vein in his temple was definitely throbbing.

"Now you're just being snide." Nothing like pointing out the obvious. "I hope you're not going to tell me to leave, because if you try it we're going to have words."

"As opposed to whatever you were having up there with Mr. Harris?" Ray's eyes, which normally flashed with gold flecks, looked more wolfish-yellow right at the moment. It dawned on me that he wasn't just angry, he was downright jealous. And I couldn't point that out, either. If I did he'd deny it and get even nastier than he had already.

I took a deep breath, squelched the desire to do an eye roll like a teenager, and went on. "Okay, you have my abject apology for getting physical with Hal in public. But I have to tell you that he honestly *was* just telling me thank-you for urging him to go to you and tell the truth. Hal and I will always have some connections with each other, but a physical relationship, or even a really deep friendship don't figure in."

While I talked Ray focused on me and he began to look less like Hondo when he's seen a coyote. His shoulders stopped bunching so tightly under his sport coat, and his expression softened just a little. "So you're the one who told him to come clean about Ms. Barnes and her overstepping her bounds with a patient? How did you figure it out in the first place?"

"It's easier to explain to you, because you saw me at Playa del Sol. Several times while I was there as a chauffeur I watched interplay between Nicole and Zoë that made me believe that something was going on."

"And you were right. You know, I think you might be good at this college counseling thing you're working on. You *are* observant."

I felt like snapping at him, telling him I was definitely more observant than some people who jumped to conclusions over a simple hug. But since the situation had just started to defuse I kept quiet on that subject. "Thank you. I try to be. And speaking of observing things, Linnette and I spent a little time at Camp Freedom yesterday." As long as Fernandez was already unhappy with me, might as well tell him everything.

He didn't explode right away so I continued. "There's a young lady down there named Sunshine who might be able to give you information that backs up Hal's version of how things happened with Zoë. She didn't know she was doing that yesterday when she talked to us, but the stories match."

"And you were down there because..." He trailed off, looking like the migraine might be coming back.

"Because we're concerned about Zoë, even if what she said implicated Hal. Her problems are a long way outside the scope of our Christian Friends group, but she could use some friends, Ray."

He still looked as though his head hurt. "So you weren't there to check out the place where we think Nicole went into the ocean, right next to Camp Freedom?"

"Not at all. In fact until just now I didn't know that was where it happened. My main reason to go to the beach involved Zoë. And I've got a second reason you'll probably like even better."

"Go on. I'm listening," he said, although his actions didn't totally match up with his words. Ray had already started scanning the crowd in the room for whatever information they could provide. His arms were crossed over his chest and his focus obviously wasn't on me anymore.

Temptation reared its ugly head to see just how wild a story I could get away with while he was only half paying attention. But since I'd been encouraging this man to get closer to God and a regular faith life for months now, I have to model good Christian behavior around him. Sometimes it takes a lot of fun out of things. "The biggest reason we went down there is that it tears me up to feel like I'm between you and Hal. It's the last place in the world I want to be, because it divides my loyalties."

Ray looked down at me, paying attention again. "I'm sorry you're in this position, Gracie Lee. It's foolish of me to think that you could stay totally out of this investigation because it involves people you're close to. Try to stay out of trouble, though."

"Believe it or not, I'm trying. The faster this all gets resolved, the quicker I can go back to a life that doesn't require so much contact with Hal."

"And the quicker you and I can talk about what happens next." He smiled, and I tried and failed to suppress a shiver up my spine. That made him smile even more. "Okay, now I feel better. You certainly didn't have that kind of reaction from hugging Harris."

"Nor do I want that kind of reaction from anybody but you," I told him softly. His eyes widened and I think the good detective nearly dropped his notebook. I don't get to take him unawares very often, but I really get a charge out of it when I do.

When we went our separate ways Ray admonished me again to be careful, but didn't say anything about leaving the visitation. That made me happy because I wanted to talk to several other people first. I saw two of them sitting in one of the upholstered benches—they were a little stark to call pews—on the right side of the room near Nicole's family.

I walked up to the pair and Catalina, one of the few people I recognized here, said hello. "You better watch your back," she said, looking more than half serious. "I think Miss Ellie tried to drill holes in it with her dirty looks a while back."

"I've just been told the same thing by the police," I told her. "And I would only feel like a bickering grade-schooler if I said 'he started it.'" I nodded toward Hal and Catalina laughed softly.

"I don't think that would matter," she said. "The

Barnes women have a tendency to see and hear things only when they bolster their own opinions on life. Otherwise, you might as well talk to a wall." I thought of Nicole, paying no attention when Hal argued that she needed to get Zoë off the property as quickly as possible. Cat's comment made me wonder what kind of experience she might have had with Nicole.

"I'll second that," said the dark-haired young woman beside Cat. "I don't think we've actually met, but I'm Monica Walker." She offered me her hand and I was struck by the softness of it. Her perfect manicure and velvety skin told me that she hadn't done a lot of duty anyplace like Playa del Sol.

"You took over for Nicole in her therapy sessions. And you're in her wedding party, so you must be a friend as well as a colleague."

Her answering smile was soft and sad. "Nicole was my roommate at Vanderbilt. I transferred after freshman year to the UC system, but we kept in touch. Then less than six months ago she joined the doctoral program I'm in and here we were back together again. We could pick up conversations like it had only been ten days apart, not ten years."

I felt a flash of envy for their friendship before I calmed a bit. Some people had that kind of deep friendship with other women in their lives—I didn't. Linnette came closest to being that kind of friend for me, but I suspected there were still a few things we kept hidden from each other. At their young age I wondered if there was anything Monica and Nicole didn't share.

"So she was already engaged to Hal when you saw her again here in California. Did she seem happy?"

Monica shrugged. "Most of the time. She was stressed some, with working on her doctorate, getting married and doing clinicals all at the same time. I'd expect that, though. I feel stressed most of the time and I'm not getting married." Her blue eyes filled with tears. "Nuts. I'm still talking about her like she's going to come back next week."

Her grief was natural enough that I felt she was telling the truth. "So that Friday night she wasn't any more upset than usual?"

Monica looked away for a moment, pressing her lips together in a thin line before she said anything else. "I've seen her a lot more upset," she finally said. That sounded as though she didn't want to say any more to me, so I talked a little more about lighter subjects and we separated.

Cat trailed behind me a couple steps as we walked toward the front of the room. Pictures of Nicole ranged around the oak console table holding an urn. Some showed a young girl in what looked like a high school senior portrait. There her dark hair was longer, styled around her face to accent model-sharp cheekbones. Otherwise Nicole at seventeen or eighteen looked younger than her age, just as she had at twenty-nine.

A photo of Nicole outside with her arm around what appeared to be a much younger Monica showed them both in a parklike setting, sun dappling through trees. They both smiled out at the camera, carefree and young.

"She was beautiful, wasn't she?" Cat said softly behind me. "She could be a real pain to work with sometimes but she always meant well." We were in front of a graduation photo now that featured the whole family, making me wonder who took the shot. I had to guess it was Nicole's college graduation, judging from the regalia she wore. Her face looked a little pinched and her smile a bit forced, but not as tight as her mother's. Her father looked calmer than any of the three women ranged around him. Paige wore the bored expression of the teenager she was, a pout pushing her lower lip out.

"How do you mean what you said, Cat? About Nicole being a pain." We both spoke in hushed tones while looking at the photos.

"Well, she was so disorganized, but so picky at the same time. She was hard on herself, and rewrote reports so much that she was always late with stuff. Nicole broke a lot of little rules, like carrying her cell phone everyplace and taking personal calls in the hospital. But she also cared about her patients, maybe too much at times, and tended to ignore her own needs."

"Not a healthy combination," I said, something tickling at the edge of my brain. Before I could figure out what was nagging at me, we were interrupted in our quiet conversation.

"That's my daughter. Isn't she the most beautiful thing you've ever seen?" Paul Barnes loomed over me, slightly unsteady on his feet. Even though I couldn't smell alcohol, his demeanor made me wonder if he'd been drinking. "And she was smart, too. Smart enough she could have gone to med school and become a psychiatrist instead of this psychology nonsense. I tried to convince her it paid a lot better, but she said she wasn't into Freud."

I angled my body to face toward Nicole's father. His handsome face looked ravaged by grief or anger, or perhaps both. "She should have moved back home instead of saying yes when that jerk asked her to marry him. She's the only one capable of holding an intelligent conversation. Now I have to listen to those two natter on about Jimmy Choo shoes and whether it's time to get their roots done."

"I'm very sorry for your loss, Dr. Barnes," Catalina said, gently taking his elbow in a gesture that made me think of how she'd handled Zoë at the hospital. "Would you like to tell me more about Nicole? I worked with her, and I was just telling..." She trailed off, eyes wide when she realized she was about to remind Nicole's father of my relationship to "the jerk."

"Gracie Lee," I put in as smoothly as possible, following Cat's lead in diverting Paul Barnes toward the front row bench. "Cat was just telling me how much she thought of your daughter."

"Everybody loved Nicole. She was valedictorian of her class at Newport Harbor High. We almost had to pay them to let the other one graduate. If it wasn't for her spot on the tennis team they wouldn't have kept her." He scowled, nodding his head toward Paige. I looked around him at Catalina, wondering how we could get him on another track. Fortunately we were spared the effort when his cell phone chirped from somewhere in the recesses of his dark suit coat.

"Excuse me. I have to take this. I only gave the number to the hospital for emergencies tonight." He walked swiftly to the side of the room, a good twenty feet from his family or any other distractions, opening the phone as he went.

"Whoa. I guess I know now where Nicole got it. Can you believe that?" Cat looked after him and I wondered if she meant his outburst with us or his answering the phone at his daughter's visitation.

"It's difficult," I told her, because both things left me stunned. Apparently I wasn't the only one; next to her mother, Paige watched him with a stricken look. I wondered how much she had heard of her father's little tirade. Any of it would have been too much.

Before I could say anything else to Cat I heard familiar voices nearby and looked up in time to see Ben introducing his grandmother to Cai Li. Apparently both generations had come in while I was busy with Dr. Barnes. This looked as if it could require immediate attention. "Looks like I may have another firestorm brewing over there, so excuse me while I go attend to some other family business."

Cat nodded distractedly, her attention still on Nicole's dad as she watched him pace. I went over to hover near Hal, his parents and the kids, unsure whether to interject myself into their discussion or not. If Lillian got at all rude I'd be in there in a heartbeat. From where I stood I could hear her talking to Cai Li. "And this is my fiancé, Ben's grandpa Roger. I hope you two stay engaged longer than we're going to, and have more luck with married life than we did the first time around." Ouch. At least she was talking to Cai Li the way she'd talk to any girl who had the temerity to snag a Harris male.

Lillian looked past the kids and saw me. "Hello, Gracie Lee. I hope you'll speak to me tonight. My son tells me I was impossibly rude to you the other day. I'm sorry you took offense at what I said."

Leave it to Hal's mother to apologize without apologizing; she only expressed her regrets at my reaction to what she had said, not the words she'd blurted out. After twenty years of Lillian Harris, this didn't surprise me. For her, it felt like a step in the right direction. At least she was trying to be nice.

In her navy dress, Lillian looked like the Southern matriarch she was and every bit of her nearly seventy years. She tried to hide stress and exhaustion with makeup, but you can only cover so much with foundation and powder. I almost felt sorry for her. "We haven't been on the best of terms for a long time, Lillian. Maybe we could try a little harder for our sons' sake." If anything would soften her, that reminder might. In the meantime both of those sons eyed us warily, while Roger had the good sense to just stand behind his "fiancée" and watch quietly.

"That's the one good reason I can think of to start over with you. Even my mother-in-law and her sister Gladys called truces for weddings and funerals and other than that they didn't speak to each other for thirty-six years." I noticed even Roger didn't rise to that one. Fortunately, neither did anybody else. I breathed a sigh of relief when the little family gathering broke up without any snarling or bloodshed.

"Do you think I could slip into the services tomorrow without causing too big a hassle for you?" I asked Hal a few minutes later.

"Do it quietly, and don't sit right at the front and you should be fine. Honestly, I'd appreciate you being there. Since the police didn't file charges against me, and I could explain to Ellie what actually went on, I think I'm sitting with the family."

"Good. Are they having any kind of graveside services, or a gathering afterward?" It felt kind of macabre to ask, knowing that everybody had been looking forward to a wedding reception such a short time before.

"Nothing graveside, because we're still debating what to do with the urn. After the memorial service here there will be a gathering for family and close friends at La Tavola."

"Was that where you were going to have the rehearsal dinner?" The elegant Italian restaurant was the kind of place Hal liked to entertain. He'd taken Ben there more than once during the school year and Ben always came home gasping about the prices.

He got teary-eyed and nodded. "No one else will acknowledge that. I guess they're afraid to mention it, as if pretending to ignore all the wedding plans will somehow make it easier on me."

"Nothing's going to make things easier on you for

a while. I think that now that you're at least cleared of charges in her death, life is as easy as it will get for some time. I'm glad that's over for you, Hal."

"Thanks again, Gracie Lee. Why don't you at least stop in at the restaurant tomorrow? Ellie may have a fit, but if she does I can smooth things over." A wry smile lifted one corner of his mouth. "If there's the smallest of silver linings to this whole horrible experience, it's that after tomorrow I don't have to be nice to Ellie Barnes anymore. I can stop at merely being civil and no one will fault me."

I smiled back at him. It wouldn't do to point out that he had gotten a much better deal on in-laws the first time around. Even after our divorce my mother had always been kinder to him than I'd ever seen Ellie. While I'd think that, now was not the time to say it, so I patted him on the arm and walked away.

For now I wanted to go home and call Linnette to talk over everything I'd heard tonight. I felt fairly sure that somewhere in the jumble of all that was the solution to how Nicole had died. However going over it all alone wasn't going to bring me closer to finding that missing piece of the puzzle.

In the lobby of the funeral parlor, or whatever a more modern native Californian would call this place, Paul Barnes still paced with a cell phone to his ear. "Look, I don't *care* what you're doing,

Brian. You promised to cover for me the next two days and you're going to do it," he said too loudly to ignore. I don't think he ever noticed Paige, ashen under her tan, as she walked past him shaking her head as she headed away from the gathering. Looking at the two of them, I wondered how long it had been since he'd really seen that particular daughter. I had a feeling it had been much too long for both their sakes.

FIFTEEN

Even talking to Linnette Monday night didn't make things any clearer for me. I told her what Monica and Cat had said about Nicole, and what I'd heard from Paul Barnes. I shared with her my interaction with Ray, and we puzzled over that together. And of course we discussed what I should wear the next day in order to be appropriate and inconspicuous.

"I'm still not sure going to the restaurant afterward is such a good idea," I told her. "But if Hal really wants me there, I'll probably do it."

Linnette sighed. "It seems like so many people are asking heavy-duty favors of you right now. I can't complain too much, since I was the first one pressuring you for something."

"Hey, nothing I've done for you put me under pressure," I reassured her. "I did it all because I wanted to. You would have done the same for me.

As far as that goes, you've already done similar things for me. If you hadn't approached me in the campus bookstore about a year and a half ago, who knows where I'd be now."

"Probably not in our Christian Friends group, anyway. And I'm so glad you're here. Now get some sleep so you don't look too washed out in that eggplant-colored sheath I'm lending you."

"Okay. I'll be over to get it about nine," I said, and after some small talk we hung up for the night. Just the act of talking to Linnette helped, even if we hadn't come to any big conclusions this time.

Thinking about everything kept me awake until I heard Ben's car pull in. He knocked on my bedroom door to tell me he was home a few moments later, as if all the noise hadn't already alerted me to that fact. Still, I was glad he checked in. He stood in the partially opened doorway for a moment and we talked for a while. His grandparents had been fairly receptive of Cai Li, much to his relief.

"I really wasn't sure about Grandma Lil," he said. "But I guess she's so wrapped up with Grandpa right now she's not worried about me marrying an Asian girl."

"I worried more about Grandpa Roger, but he was cool, too," I said. "Right now he seems as focused on Grandma as she is on him."

"I know. I can't decide if it's really romantic or very, very creepy." Ben sounded so confused he made me want to crack up. Maybe at nineteen it was inconceivable that folks in their sixties and seventies could still feel romantic about each other. Personally I hope that when I'm Roger and Lillian's age I still feel capable of a romantic relationship. By then Ben should be a little more comfortable with the idea. Since he'd be middle-aged himself by that time, we can only hope.

We talked a bit about his plans for Tuesday, which included picking up Cai Li and meeting Hal at the memorial service. Ben worried a little about his lack of a suit, but I tried to reassure him that his dark pants and shirt, along with his all-purpose navy blazer would work well. "I can't hang around at La Tavola for long afterward, because they want me to work at one," he said.

I thought he was doing the right thing by supporting his dad during the service, and then going to work later in the day, and I told him so. After a little talk about less serious issues he told me good-night and I finally dozed off, listening to him rattle around in his room.

Tuesday morning came very quickly. By eight-thirty I stood on Linnette's front porch with a couple of lattes and two scones. She let me in and we chatted and ate breakfast while I tried on her dress. "With the weight you've lost you probably fit in this, too, don't you?" In the mirrored closet door of her bedroom, I had to admit that I didn't look quite as inconspicuous as I'd wanted, but it was very attractive in an understated way.

"I guess I probably would. I honestly hadn't considered it." Linnette smiled. "Anyway, I think it looks better on you. Once you bring it back, I'll try it again. I'm not sure how it will go with this particular red that my hair is tinted right now, but it's worth a try."

I hugged her, my spirits lifted. "I think you must be on the way back. Look at us. We're talking about hair and clothes and you've actually eaten most of that scone."

Linnette giggled, a wonderful sound. "I guess I better go easy on that if I want to fit into that dress. But you're right, Gracie Lee. I feel like I'm on the way back. It's a very good feeling."

With my shoes and Linnette's dress, which had a short-sleeved jacket to match, I felt like I might be okay at the memorial service. The drive back to Dodd and Sons didn't take long. I checked my lipstick in the vanity mirror of the car and sat there for a few minutes, not wanting to be among the first to enter the service.

Once several other cars had pulled into the lot and their occupants had gone inside, I joined them.

Nothing much had changed since last night except for the flowers being moved around some to group around the low console table holding the urn. A podium with a microphone replaced the chairs in the front of the room. Ellie, Paige and Paul Barnes were standing in front of the first bench on the right side, talking to a middle-aged couple who didn't look familiar.

No one in the family looked as if they'd gotten much rest overnight. Ellie's outfit made me think that perhaps everyone had gone with the "rehearsal dinner" theme today, wearing the outfits they had probably bought for that occasion. Her tailored blue-green dress and duster style jacket of fabric that looked like silk would have been much more festive with different jewelry.

Dr. Barnes, of course, wore another dark suit. I imagined that as a successful plastic surgeon he probably had a collection of them. He looked like the kind of man who owned a current tuxedo, too.

Very near Nicole's family stood her "other" family, Hal and his parents arrayed just outside the group talking to the Barneses. Hal looked even more tired than Nicole's parents, if that was possible. He seemed to have far more silver at his temples than I remembered from just two weeks ago, and I wondered if the events of the last fourteen days had aged him that much. That or he'd been touching up his hair before, and without Nicole here to remind him, he'd stopped doing it. In either case his graying temples added to the air of sorrow around him. I felt glad that I'd agreed to come for his sake. If Ellie didn't like my presence, I hoped she'd keep that opinion to herself.

From a distance Hal's parents also looked older than usual, although they supported each other more than I'd ever seen, Lillian's hand on Roger's arm and Roger standing protectively close to her. I felt glad that they'd been able to get back together, and I hoped that they were in some kind of marital counseling back in Tennessee. With everything they'd gone through and put each other through, they were going to need to do some serious talking for all of this to work out this time.

As I stood in the back of the room considering where to sit, Ben and Cai Li walked in. Ben looked handsome in his outfit and Cai's dark dress might have been a bit shorter than I would have chosen, but otherwise was just right for the occasion. They made a beautiful couple and for the first time I let myself daydream, just a little, about what their children might look like. That daydream didn't last long, because I shook myself out of it quickly. It was time to find a seat. I chose one of the left-hand benches about halfway back. Soft music played as background for the several conversations going on around me, and I let myself sit and center down in prayer for the shortened life of this young woman and the pain that her early death had caused her family.

As I prayed the room began to fill up. I began to wonder who was working at Playa del Sol today, because the bulk of the staff that I remembered seeing from my trips there appeared to be here. Cat and Monica sat directly behind the Barnes family while Hal was flanked by his parents on one side and Ben and Cai Li on the other. A few people that looked closer in age to Nicole's parents might have been her father's colleagues, and I imagined there was a fair amount of extended family here, as well.

Closer to where I sat, about halfway from the front rows there were many younger people who either worked with Nicole or probably went to school with her. I had no idea how large or close knit her doctoral program in psychology was. Somewhere in the crowd her professors more than likely made up one of the groups of professional-looking folks talking softly over the formless New Age music.

Before long the music began to gather tune and sound more purposeful, and several people gathered to sit in the chairs set out facing the benches, close to the speaker's podium. While plenty of flowers surrounded the urn, nowhere were there definite symbols of any specific religion in the way of banners, crosses or anything else. White candles flickered in stands tied with pale ribbon, all of it lending an air of poignancy to the occasion.

The memorial service turned out to be much more "inspirational" than religious. California has a host of churches and religious institutions that I'd never heard of before coming out here, and the woman presiding over today's service was of one of those faith expressions. God was mentioned as a creator spirit in a sort of vague way. The whole proceedings made me wonder what Hal and Nicole's marriage ceremony would have sounded like.

Friends and colleagues got up and said things about Nicole. She was remembered as a kind, conscientious person who might have made quite a mark in her profession had she lived. Hal talked briefly, managing to hold himself together for most of his speech, making my heart ache for him. Even though any romantic feelings for him had disappeared years ago, I still understood the man better than I did most of the male population. I knew that talking about Nicole under these circumstances in front of this many people had to be tearing him apart.

The minister or presider or whatever she might be called then spoke for a while, and it was fairly apparent that while she might have known the Barnes family in a peripheral kind of way, she hadn't had much contact with Nicole. Nothing she said about her had the depth that Hal's remarks or even Nicole's fellow grad students had shown. I found myself getting weepy wondering how I'd be remembered if I died at this point in my life. Who could say something substantial about me? And how much of it would be good?

While I'd been in my little reverie they'd played a piece of music that probably had a great deal of significance for Nicole and others her age, but that was totally unfamiliar to me. Then her father stepped to the podium, clearing his throat several times before he could speak. "From the moment that she was born, Nicole was the brightest spot in my life," he began. I decided then and there the man had all the typical people skills of a surgeon. Here he stood in front of his wife and his living daughter and basically told them they were second best. He continued to go on about Nicole—her sunny disposition as a child, her determination to succeed academically and her dreams to become a doctor. I hoped he and Lillian would be sitting near each other at La Tavola so they could compare notes on their brilliant kids. He hadn't seemed to think much of Hal, and I was fairly positive that Hal's mom would have said that while Nicole might have come closer than I did, she wasn't good enough for Lillian's pride and joy.

Listening to all of this kept teasing an idea from

my brain. I wanted to pull a pen from my purse and write something on the back of the service bulletin just to remind me to ask a few questions at the gathering afterward. That would be rude, though, and call attention to me. As it was I just listened intently to Paul Barnes continue to praise his dead daughter while the living one moved ever closer to her mother's side.

After Paul finished speaking there was another song, one that I almost recognized. The lovely young soloist sang perfectly with tears softly running down her cheeks. Once more the horrible irony of the day overwhelmed me. This girl must have bought her dress and learned her piece to sing at a wedding and instead she was performing at a funeral. Many of the people there had joined the singer in tears by the time she finished and the older woman in her dark suit closed the proceedings. The family led the way out of the "chapel" and the rest of us followed slowly. Outside the June gloom of the morning had burned off into brilliant sunshine, mocking the mood of the service.

Before I reached my car Ben caught up with me. "Dad sent me over to ask if you are coming to the restaurant. I think he really wants you there." My son looked like he'd been crying, and the handkerchief that had been tucked into his breast pocket was gone.

"Yes, I'll come. Tell him I won't stay for hours

because I don't think it would be right, but I'll be there for a while." I straightened Ben's collar and patted him on the shoulder. "I've probably already told you this, but I'm proud of the way you've been there for your dad lately." Unspoken between us was the thought that Hal might not have been able to give Ben the same kind of support had the situation demanded.

"Thanks, Mom." He looked down at me and gave me a brief hug. "I don't think I'm the only guy who learned to be a man from watching his mom handle life." He dropped a quick kiss somewhere in the region of the top of my head and loped back across the parking lot toward the building. If I'd been proud of him before, I was, as my Granny Jo would have said, "fit to bust" watching him now.

La Tavola was the kind of place where alcoves often held celebrities having a quiet dinner and the chef was rumored to be so hot that he was next up for a show on the cable food channel. Whatever the trendy ingredients of the moment and cooking styles on the cutting edge were, whether it was roasted pumpkin seeds, goat cheese croutons or things like fondue—so uncool that it was cool again—they would show up here first.

I'd never been through the front doors before, not being willing to drop a week's pay on lunch.

Today the smoked-glass doors had elegant hand-lettered signs informing the regular clientele that lunch service would be limited to the patio due to a private party.

Inside the atmosphere was somber and the bar darkened. The trendy Tuscan decor lent itself to the quiet mood and the staff had obviously been well-informed of the nature of the gathering because they went about their work with little conversation.

Tables for eight ranged around the main room of the restaurant, heavy damask tablecloths further adding to the noise-dampening quality of the place. Across the room Hal stood, having loosened his tie a bit and draped his dark gray suit jacket over the back of a chair. In the low light he didn't look much older than Ben until I got close enough to see the new lines on either side of his mouth. "Ben said you were coming. I appreciate it, Gracie Lee."

"Hey, I told you I'd try to make it," I told him. "I hope you get time to eat something. You look like it's been days since you had a real meal."

His smile didn't reach his eyes. "Now you sound like my mother. I've even turned down her offers to cook chicken and dumplings so you know I've had no appetite."

"That's pretty understandable. Try to eat something anyway, just to keep yourself going. Is it hard to get into the habit of doing your own meals with Nicole gone?"

He shrugged. "Not that much different. We went out a lot of nights, even with that granite-and-cherry kitchen big enough to have a party in. We did a lot of sushi."

That was hard for me to wrap my mind around, but I didn't press. "And when you stayed home?" I asked.

Hal looked off in the middle distance, remembering what must have been better times. "Nicole mostly fixed herself a salad or had one of those dinky cups of nonfat yogurt. She'd bring in all kinds of stuff for me, but any time lately I mentioned grilling a steak or having pizza or anything she clucked about fitting into that backless wedding dress."

The idea I'd had before grew stronger with every word Hal spoke. The picture of Nicole in her white lab coat the day I'd met her at Playa del Sol flashed in my memory; I could see her frail wrists poking out from the cuffs of the coat, and the way she'd absently toyed with her engagement ring.

Hal stopped talking, looking like he'd run out of steam. "Well, I don't want to get Ellie mad at you, so I'll move on to a table someplace before she gets here," I told him. "I'll come back and say goodbye before I leave."

He nodded with a distracted air, scanning the room in case his almost in-laws came through the door. I hadn't seen them yet, but I did notice Cat and Monica standing near the buffet table of salads, talking softly with a third young woman I thought I recognized from the hospital.

Once they had gotten plates and the group dispersed I went quickly through the line myself, putting food on my plate so that I fit in with the rest, then going over to the table where Monica and the nurse sat together. They asked me to join them and I did, picking at my food for a little while, waiting for the right moment to ask them a few things. It came quickly when Cat excused herself to get up for a moment.

"Maybe this is terrible, but I've always heard this place has the best tiramisu in the county and I'll never come here again on my own. Do you two want anything from the dessert table?"

Monica and I both turned her down. Once Cat had left the table I leaned closer to Monica. She had gray-blue circles under her eyes that her makeup couldn't quite conceal. "Do you feel like you made it through today all right?" I asked her. "This has to have been a difficult day."

"It has been, but I'm getting through okay." Even in this slightly dark corner of the restaurant, I could see the stress on Monica's face.

"I'd like to ask you a question, and I'll understand if you choose not to answer," I told her. "After looking at all the pictures of Nicole last night, it made me wonder. Did she have an eating disorder when you roomed together at Vanderbilt?"

Monica looked at me silently for a moment and I felt sure that she was ready to shut me down. Then she looked away and spoke softly. "Not so much at first. She told me she'd gotten some treatment in high school, but that being away from her family she was okay. And she was, until about a week before finals. Then she probably dropped five pounds in as many days, and she was the only girl on the floor who hadn't gained the Freshman Fifteen. On her you could really notice when she stopped eating out of stress."

"The pictures seemed to show a pattern. She looked thinner and a bit distracted in every big 'event' photo that involved her, and not nearly as much otherwise."

Monica nodded. "That was Nicole. Always sure she could control everything, wanted life to be perfect. Somewhere along the line her brain bought into the idea that perfect meant thin, and her eating was the one thing she could control when everything else fell apart."

I went with my gut instinct and asked the big

question. "When did she start doing that again? And did her parents know?"

Monica's eyes filled with tears. "I told her she ought to tell them but Nicole said no way. She talked her therapist into sending her to somebody they knew who would prescribe some meds for her and she just kept on going. I thought maybe she should postpone the wedding if everything was that nuts for her, but she didn't go for that idea, either."

I couldn't tell Monica just how much her friend actually had gone for that idea, although it had done her little good. "So you don't think her family knew this time that she'd needed a doctor?"

"Probably not. And I know Hal didn't. She made me swear not to tell him, even the day she almost passed out at work."

There are sometimes I hated to be right and this was one of them. "Did anybody else know besides you and her doctors, do you think?"

Monica's forehead wrinkled in thought. "Cat, maybe. Nicole confided in her as much as she did in me, I think. But otherwise she would have kept it quiet. If the hospital would have found out they might have pulled her off group therapy rotation and she needed the clinical hours to finish up her degree."

Before we could say more Cat came back with a small plate in one hand and a coffee cup in the other. "Tiramisu and ricotta-almond cannoli, too.

And I brought enough cookies to share." We stopped our conversation for a moment and each took a cookie from the plate as Cat sat down. Right now a little sugar sounded as good as anything else. If I didn't already feel so jumpy I might have looked for a cup of real Italian espresso to go with it all. Maybe they had decaf.

SIXTEEN

I ended up getting decaf cappuccino for Monica and myself, and then sat and listened to her and Cat talk a little more about Nicole. Cat asked Monica what Nicole had been like as a roommate. "I mean, could she find anything in her half of the room? Did it look like her cubicle at the hospital?"

"Worse. By October I'd bought this special bowl that was bright red, and I put it on top of my dresser. Not her dresser, but mine. And every time she came in the room I *made* her put her keys in it because I was already tired of the hour-long searches and calling the residence hall service that made keys."

"Which was up to you because half the time she didn't have a phone, right?"

Monica nodded. "Right. She didn't ever lose the phone, but she always forgot to charge it or she couldn't find the charger. At least she got over that part."

Cat wrinkled her nose, emphasizing the pale freckles across her cheeks. "Yeah. It's hard to forget a phone that rings every three minutes. Even that last night, it never stopped ringing."

This sounded like new information. "Who was she talking to?" Surely Hal didn't keep that close a watch on her. He might be a type-A neat freak but he wasn't controlling in other ways.

"Paige," they both said together.

"Her sister felt really bad about not coming with us that night, and she must have called Nicole seven or eight times," Monica explained. "I told her to just turn the phone off, but she wouldn't do it."

"She wanted to talk to Paige," Cat added. "There was something going on that she wasn't telling us. Monica might have been her best friend, but Paige always ranked higher."

Okay, that surprised me, and I said so. "From what I've seen of the parents I would have thought the girls would be at each other's throats."

Monica smiled. "You don't have a sister, do you?"

"Nope. I'm an only child," I admitted.

"Kids whose parents play favorites either compete their whole lives or band together in sympathy. Nicole and Paige stuck together. But even Paige didn't know that Nicole was taking anti-anxiety drugs to try to combat the anorexia."

Cat took another sip of coffee, looking thoughtful. "That's one thing we knew that her family didn't. Nicole's biggest problem might have been that she didn't let anybody in on all her secrets. I think she and Hal might have had a fight before she left the house that night, but Nicole pretended everything was great. She kept tossing down Kamikaze shots fast enough to worry both of us." She looked over at Monica. "I know I paid the bartender at that second place to leave the vodka out of hers. I was afraid she was going to get sick."

Monica shook her head, looking down at the table. "I think we were both trying to keep her from drinking. Why didn't it work?"

Cat suddenly looked more somber. "Maybe it did. Even though she swore she was going straight home after we poured coffee down her at your place, I heard her talking to Paige again in the car right before she left. What if they met up somewhere?"

Monica rocked back in her chair, and I felt cold fingers climb my spine. This could be the missing piece of the puzzle. Perhaps Nicole's secrecy and need to be perfect were the ultimate causes of her death. I looked around the room, scanning each table from our quiet spot with its great vantage point. Twenty or thirty others gathered at different areas, but I couldn't find the person I wanted most.

Actually, there were a few people I wanted to find, and my first look around didn't spot any of them. Not only was Paige absent but I didn't see Hal anywhere, or Ellie Barnes. I told myself that could mean the three of them were finally having their differences out somewhere, but the atmosphere of the room was still too subdued for there to be that kind of argument going on. On a hunch, I went into the ladies' room and found Ellie at the long vanity mirror sitting on one of the upholstered stools where women sat to fix their makeup.

"What on earth are you doing here?" She glared into the mirror as I stood behind her. "Don't you have the decency to let our family grieve in peace?"

"I'm sorry my presence upsets you, Mrs. Barnes, but Hal asked me to come and I said I would. He loved your daughter very much and I think he needs all the support he can get right now." We seemed to be the only two people here. "Actually I'm getting ready to leave, and I wanted to talk to Paige first."

"Well, she's not with me. I haven't seen her since we got here. We had to almost manhandle her to get her into her father's car for the trip to the restaurant. He was barely parked when she leaped out."

"Did that surprise you?" I probably should have kept my mouth shut, but as usual, my tongue was running ahead of my common sense.

"Not really. I've tried to tell her that her father doesn't mean half of what he says, and that right now he's just beside himself, anyway. But Paige has always been sensitive where her father's concerned."

That might be the understatement of the year. "After talking to Cat and Monica I'm a little concerned about your daughter, Ellie. Do you think she's still here somewhere?"

"Of course. We all came together and she doesn't have enough money with her to get back to Newport Beach otherwise. Even somebody in as good a shape as Paige wouldn't leave on foot dressed like she was."

"I hope you're right," I told her, my worry growing with the minute. I had a funny feeling about all of this, and whether he would believe me or not, it was time to tell Ray. I left Ellie still looking in the mirror and went out into the main room to find my favorite detective.

Of course nobody had seen him in at least fifteen minutes. "I think he took a phone call about something, and then he left quickly." I got the information from what I thought was the least likely source, my former mother-in-law. When I couldn't find Ray I'd started looking for Hal. Naturally he'd gone into the manager's office, according to his mother, to settle the bill. When I mentioned I'd actually been looking for the detective she surprised me by telling me where he'd gone, as well.

Given her supreme position as queen busybody,

I should have known Lillian would keep tabs on virtually everybody here. "How about Nicole's dad?" I asked her, fairly sure she'd have the answer this time.

"He had quite a little talk with his other daughter about fifteen minutes ago, she stormed out of here, and he went to the bar." Lillian's lip curled to tell me what she'd thought of all that. "I expect he's still there."

Since Paul Barnes was the only person I wanted to find who seemed to be available, I looked into the bar. He sat there staring into a highball glass as if it held the secrets of the universe. "I'm looking for Paige," I told him, not feeling like making small talk.

"Good luck. She's probably past Calabasas by now," he said, referring to a town about eight miles away on the 101 freeway. "We had an argument and she stormed out. I didn't think much of it until I went back to the table to get my suit jacket. My keys are gone. The little twit better not wrap that Mercedes around a tree. It's not paid for yet."

I stood there openmouthed, unable to say anything in response to his awful remarks. "Does this mean you haven't told the police that she's gone and took your car?"

"How could I? The only officer present left before Paige did. It's true, that saying. There's never a cop around when you need one."

There was never one on the phone, either, as I discovered shortly. Ray's number put me straight to voice mail, and I gave him a brief message about where I was going and why. Still not finding Hal, I told his mother I was leaving, and left before she could argue with me. Paige had triggered my "mom radar" in a big way, and I drove as fast as I could north on the freeway, away from Calabasas but toward Paige, I believed.

I kept a running prayer going most of the time I drove north to Ventura. I didn't know whether to hope I was wrong about all my assumptions or that I was right but in time to catch Paige before anything happened.

The beach parking lot wasn't very full on a Tuesday afternoon. Some schools were still in session, so there weren't tons of moms and kids there yet. This wasn't the most popular of the beaches anyway; most families chose a more parklike stretch closer to the pier where lifeguards and concession stands dotted the landscape with regularity.

Here most of the beachgoers were seagulls and ground rats. I hadn't known about the rats the first couple times I roamed the beach. Lexy took great glee one day in pointing them out, watching me almost levitate at the thought of sharing the sand with them.

A black Mercedes with the driver's side door open told me my hunch had been right. Before I could get the car parked and find Paige my phone rang. "Where are you? And tell me that wherever it is, you're not there alone." Ray wasn't yelling, but he sounded plenty upset.

"I'm at the beach parking lot at the end of Oak Street and I didn't think I had time to wait for anybody else. I was right, too, because Paige is here. She took her father's car and drove here to the beach where she and Nicole were the night Nicole died."

"I'm not even going to ask how you put all that twisted logic together. At least promise me you'll stay in the car until we get somebody there."

"No way. I'm not going to sit here and watch that girl hurt herself." I could see Paige now, huddled on a rock outcrop a little way down the beach. While I watched, there was a flash of metal. "Oh, no."

"What? What's happening? Gracie Lee…"

"I'm going to hang up and go over there. Tell dispatch to send the closest officers you can. And paramedics, too." Ignoring Ray's protests I pushed the red button that ended the call, and then turned off my phone so Paige wouldn't hear it ringing. The realization that Linnette's dress didn't have any pockets made me want to swear. I grabbed the car keys and my phone, launched myself out of the car and kicked off my sandals when I got to the place where the gravel parking lot met the sand sloping downward to the beach. Even barefoot I couldn't run well in the sand, but at least this way I'd make a little more speed. And right now a few seconds might make a difference.

I slid a little on the incline, glad that it wasn't any steeper. "Paige?" I called her name softly as I got closer to her, not wanting to startle her. "Paige, are you okay?" Of course she wasn't okay, I chastised myself. A black leather messenger bag laid sprawled open next to her, various contents strewed on the sand. Looking at all of it I realized the gravity of Paige taking her father's car. Even a plastic surgeon would carry a medical bag with him, and Paul Barnes might have been a lousy father but he seemed to be a well-prepared doctor. Several open pill bottles lay on their sides, and implements of various kinds were scattered with them.

Paige sobbed, not looking up even when I called her name. The flash of metal I'd seen was from a scalpel and a thin line of blood trailed down her left hand from a cut on the inside of her wrist. "I am such a pathetic loser," she wailed, waving the blade for emphasis. "I can't even kill myself. The pills made me barf and I can't cut deep enough to bleed to death. I can kill my sister, but I can't kill myself."

Her right hand relaxed in her lap and she

stopped jabbing at her wrist, but didn't let go of the scalpel. I breathed a silent prayer and sat down about four feet from her rock perch, settling into the gritty sand as much as the slim skirt of the sheath would let me. Right now I was grateful for the back slit of the dress that I'd debated as being too daring earlier. "You didn't kill your sister. At least you didn't mean for her to die, did you?" Over the noise of the surf I could hear sirens and hoped that Paige wouldn't panic even more because of them.

She finally looked up at me, eyes wild and makeup smeared in dark trails down her face. "What does that matter? She's dead, and I did it. Just because I didn't mean for her to die won't bring her back."

"No, I know it won't. But why don't you tell me about it? Maybe if you talk about what happened we can figure out a way to explain it to..." Only then did I see the corner I'd painted myself into.

"To who? The police who already nearly arrested her geeky fiancé for killing her? My mom, who is ready to kill somebody over all of this anyway? My dad, who looks at me and thinks the wrong kid died? Who would possibly listen if I tried to explain what happened?"

I took a deep breath, wanting to move closer but

knowing it wasn't right yet. "I'll listen. And I'd go with you to any of those other people, because I think I know what must have happened already. You met Nicole here that night after her bachelorette party, didn't you?"

She looked out onto the expanse of gray-green water in front of us. "Yeah, I did. Can you believe I didn't go with them because I was out on a date? And the guy wasn't worth it, either. I ditched him when Nic said she wanted to talk, and I met her here because she said she was too tired to drive any farther."

"What happened when you got here?"

"She was a mess. She like, never drank, but she'd been drinking that night. And she was really upset. She was going on about how she hated her life and how she wanted to walk away from everything and just disappear or something. It made me so mad. I mean, Nic always got all the attention." She wore a childish pout that made me wonder how long Paige had felt abandoned by her family.

"I heard your parents say she was valedictorian of her class in high school. That must have been hard to follow."

"Everything Nic did was hard to follow." Paige was jabbing the scalpel in the sand now as she talked. "Whether she was Miss 'Most Likely to

Succeed' or 'Most Likely to Die of Starvation' I could have won an Academy award or got hit by a bus and nobody would notice."

"Did she tell you she was being treated for her eating disorder?" The sirens were close now, and then stopped abruptly, making me will myself to keep my attention focused on Paige and not look toward the parking lot.

"No. Even I wouldn't have given her some of my stuff to calm her down if I'd known. But she took it! And washed it down with my Coke before I could tell her there was rum in it. I thought she was dead, honest!"

"Is that why you put her in the water?"

Paige nodded. "I really thought it would look better that way. If her car was found at home and her body in the ocean, somebody else would get blamed for her death."

"Like Hal?"

"Maybe. He deserved it, the way he got her all upset. And she never moved again, even when I put her in the water," she said, trying to convince me again that she was 'only' disposing of her sister's body.

"I believe you," I told her. Before I could say more a car door slammed and Paige looked up, startled. Eyes wide, I expected her to spring up and run, and got up on my knees to try to catch her.

Instead she lunged for me and grabbed me in a surprisingly strong grip, pulling me even nearer.

"Don't come any closer or I'll kill her," she screeched, making my ears ring. In this position on the sand I couldn't pull away from her in time, and then her left arm slammed across my neck in a chokehold. The coppery smell of blood from her wrist almost made me gag. Two young uniformed officers stood ten feet from us, stilled by her threat.

The next few minutes stretched out to an incredible length. I could hear every noise, from Paige's ragged breathing behind me to the gulls wheeling overhead. One of the officers spoke into a crackling radio, and then lowered his hand. "We won't come closer. There's an ambulance already on the way, but I'll tell them to stay in the parking lot, okay?"

"Just keep them away. Keep them all away." I could feel Paige's body trembling, but her grip on my throat didn't let up. I could breathe, just barely, but not talk without effort. On the right side of my neck I could feel that metal blade and I tried to stay as still as possible so that it didn't slice into my skin.

On the parking lot the heavy crunch of gravel indicated the ambulance pulling up, and the pale young officer spoke into his handheld radio again, taking several steps back from Paige as he did so.

His words were soft enough that I couldn't hear what he said over the waves on the beach.

"A couple more officers are coming down. I can't stop everybody," the deputy warned as several car doors opened and closed just far enough away that we couldn't see the vehicles. There was a flurry of activity down the slope to where he and his partner still stood and I could feel Paige's grip tighten. Sweat was making my eyes sting by now and my leg muscles felt like they were on fire.

The sweat mixed with tears when I saw that Ray was one of the three people who'd come on the scene. I'd never seen him that pale beneath his olive complexion. I tried to communicate as much as I could to him without speaking, and it seemed as if he was doing the same thing.

Beside him was a woman I hadn't ever seen before. I prayed she was a psychologist or a hostage negotiator, and I thanked God silently that Ray or someone had thought to bring a woman along. Paige wasn't likely to respond well to a group made up only of men.

"Miss Barnes? Paige?" Ray's voice was firm, but quiet. "I'm going to walk toward you, but only a couple more steps so that I'm sure you can hear me. And I'm bringing Jackie with me." He motioned toward the woman on his right, who lowered her head slightly in greeting.

"Don't come any closer!" Paige's voice rose in fear and I could feel the scalpel press into the side of my throat with a sting.

Ray raised both of his hands, palms out toward her. The woman he'd introduced as Jackie stopped any forward motion, as well, and focused on Paige as though no one else was around. "You don't want to hurt her, Paige. Right now we can straighten everything out, but not if you hurt anyone."

"How about if I kill someone? Like her?" The pressure of her arm across my throat lifted me backward almost off my knees and I fought not to slide to my right where the blade would go deeper.

"Please, Paige, don't do that." Ray's voice held a note I had never heard before and the look on Jackie's face told me his outburst wasn't in the script. "We don't want anyone to end up dead today. If you hurt Gracie Lee, one of us will shoot you. And if that happens, your parents will lose their only daughter. And despite what you might think right now, that would destroy them."

"They love you," Jackie said, her eyes showing that she felt back on track again. "And they want to tell you that. Nobody wants any more pain or suffering for them, or for you, or for anybody today. We can help make everything all right if you'll just let us a little closer." Jackie's words were almost pleading without sounding weak. She didn't make any moves to come closer.

"I have another reason I don't want you to hurt that woman you've taken hostage, Miss Barnes." Ray's voice drew my attention, and it seemed to draw Paige's, as well, because her grip on me relaxed just a little bit and I was able to shift away from her right hand and the bite of the scalpel. "If you hurt her, I won't get to tell her how much she means to me, just like your parents wouldn't get a chance to tell you how much you mean to them. It would be so wrong if we've all waited too late to do something so important."

He inched forward about a quarterstep. "Jackie is trained in negotiations. If you want her to, she could sit down with you and your parents and the sheriff's department."

Jackie nodded slightly, and I kept praying silently that Paige's attention was drawn to her and not to Ray, moving ever so slightly closer while Jackie talked. "It's my job. If you tell me what happened I can see that they understand that it was all a mistake. You really didn't mean for any of it to happen, did you?"

"They'll never believe that," Paige said, voice flat and hollow. I felt her muscles tense and decided that my only chance to live was to do the unexpected. Trusting an instinct that had to be

God-given, because it was against my better judgment, I went as limp as possible, dead weight against her body. My move unbalanced us both and Paige tumbled backward. The sand exploded with activity and in a flash someone dragged her away from me.

Noise erupted from officers, from radios and paramedics charging down the little hill from the parking lot. Ray knelt above me, his hand pressed on the side of my throat. After a moment I got my dry mouth to form words. "Did you mean what you said before, or was it just a distraction?"

"Every word. But don't say any more and don't move until we make sure that cut is taken care of." It was only then that I felt the warmth of liquid under his fingers and the bright sky above me darkened. Whether I fainted or was just overwhelmed by the activity around me I'll never know.

Some people say there are only two real prayers; "Please, please, please," and "Thank you, thank you, thank you." As I slid into a fog, I felt the shift from the first to the second as the tide and my pulse roared in my ears.

SEVENTEEN

"Next time, somebody else is definitely going first," I said, trying to make somebody smile Wednesday night. Our Christian Friends group had gotten much too serious as I told them everything about my encounter with Paige.

"I'll second that motion," Linnette said. "Can't somebody else come up with a crisis so Gracie Lee doesn't feel the need to have one every time?"

"Hey, I'm done with mine for the present, except that I owe you a new dress," I told her. "Even the best cleaner in Rancho Conejo isn't going to be able to get all the stains out of the one you lent me." Not when the stains included blood, salty mud from the beach and other assorted stuff from the inside of an ambulance.

"Forget it. I'll just borrow whatever you buy for the kids' wedding," Linnette told me, her smile looking a little forced.

"You'll have to wait awhile, then. They decided to back off on the engagement for now."

"Gee, I wonder why?" Lexy's voice held a note of sarcasm. "You think it had anything to do with what they've seen in the last few weeks?"

She'd guessed it in one try. When I got home from the hospital, Ben and Cai Li had given me the news first thing. "Ben phrased it very bluntly. He said he had no desire to be planning a double wedding with his grandparents, and that focusing on school was looking better and better to both of them."

"What's going to happen to Paige?" Heather asked from the chair where she'd been grading papers and listening at the same time. Even with her toddler at home with Sandy, Heather felt the need to multitask.

"I'm not sure yet. I'm not about to ask Ray anything that he couldn't tell the rest of the general public. Right now she's being treated at Playa del Sol, along with Zoë." The one thing I'd found out was that sheriff's department prisoners who needed mental health care went to a locked part of the hospital there. "I imagine Paige's father is trying to get her transferred to some private facility in Orange County."

"Well, good luck to him on that one," Lexy muttered. As a lawyer she'd have the most insight of any of us into that, even if she did specialize in entertainment. "So how long until you get those stitches out?"

My hand went to my neck self-consciously. "About a week. And there are only three of them."

Linnette shuddered. "Only three. You do realize how lucky you are, don't you?"

"Let's call it blessed," I told her. "I don't know if I've ever felt God's presence as strongly as I did on that beach."

"Fine. Then maybe you can lead us in prayer tonight. It will give you practice for your trip to Las Vegas."

I groaned, but nodded. I still couldn't believe that Linnette had talked me into going through training to be a Christian Friends leader. Spending a week at a training session in Nevada's "Sin City" wasn't my idea of a great time, but I'd felt such an urging to agree to it that I couldn't ignore the Call.

An hour later the cool night air felt welcome on my face. "Somebody ought to give you a ticket," I told the driver of the silver sedan that met me at the red-painted curb in front of the church building.

"Yeah, I'll issue myself one," Ray said, rolling his eyes as I got into the front seat. "Right after I give you one for reckless endangerment."

"I don't think you can do that when the person in danger is the person you're giving the ticket to," I told him. He'd already told me what he'd thought of my actions, the day before at the hospital. Since I couldn't argue much, I'd given in to his insistence that he accompany me for a few days any time I left the apartment.

He leaned over and kissed me on the cheek. "Maybe I could try anyway. It wouldn't do any good, though, would it?"

"Probably not." Nicole's death had made me resolve one thing—if I had been honest in most situations before, I was determined to be honest all the time now. Secrets could kill people.

"You up for ice cream, or should I take you straight home?" Ray paused at the Chapel's entrance to the street while I made up my mind.

"Ice cream first, then take me home."

"Good. I want you to explain to me again why the mention of keys and cell phones made you realize what was happening with Paige, and why you were so sure she caused her sister's death."

"I'll try, but there's a lot of intuition involved and I know how you hate that."

"Not as much as I love you, Gracie Lee." I rolled down my window to let the breeze ruffle my hair, as I silently prayed that same prayer I'd prayed the day before. *"Thank you, thank you, thank you."* I may never get tired of it again.

* * * * *

Dear Reader,

Some books are harder to write than others, and this one proved to be one of those that was difficult for me to write. I hope the extra effort shows through and you enjoy Gracie Lee's adventure. Two of the questions writers are always asked is whether their stories are based on their own experiences, and if the characters are real. For me the answers to those questions can't always be answered with a straight yes or no. My own experiences are what shape my writing, and people who have read several of my books know that I've got a heart for those with mental and emotional illness and their families, because that's where I feel called to ministry as a Christian. I don't base any character on one real person for a lot of reasons, ranging from ethics to the belief that as a writer it's a lot more fun to create fictional people than describe real ones.

For those who ask if the Christian Friends are real, the answer is an easy no. However, if you're looking for good, real ministry groups in your local church or community, I can never say enough good things about Stephen Ministry and ChristCare small-group ministry. As a Stephen Leader for close to a decade, I recommend their services without hesitation based on my own experience and the testimony of others. These ministries happen in congregations and hospitals in all kinds of Christian environments across the country, and if you need distinctively Christian caregiving, it's my hope that you can find a group in your community.

Blessings,

Lynn Bulock

QUESTIONS FOR DISCUSSION

1. The theme verse for this book comes from 1 Corinthians 13, a passage read during many weddings. Look at that book of the Bible together. What do you think is the most important thing Paul tells us about love?

2. Do you know anyone who struggles with depression and issues of faith, as Linnette does? How are you a support as a friend or family member to that person?

3. Relationships, and marriages, particularly are at the heart of this book. What do you think Hal and Nicole's marriage would have been like if they had married?

4. What do you think of Ben and Cai Li's decision to marry before either turned twenty-one? What would you add to the advice their parents gave them?

5. Sometimes it takes a crisis for people to tell someone else what they mean to them. Have you ever been in that kind of crisis? Share your experience with the group if you're comfortable.

6. Nicole's family seems to play favorites among parents and children. What kinds of problems does this create for a family?

7. Does God ever play favorites among His children? Explain your answer.

8. What kind of message did Roger and Lillian send to their children and grandchildren in their decision about remarriage? If a friend asked you how to handle a similar situation, what would you tell her?

9. Nicole made a decision to let a patient come home with her, a clear violation of the rules and ethics of the place where she worked. How do you decide what to do in a situation where you feel the rules are wrong?

10. How could Nicole have helped Zoe in a way that would have been healthier for both of them?

Love Inspired® SUSPENSE

TITLES AVAILABLE NEXT MONTH

Don't miss these four stories in August

MURDER BY MUSHROOM by Virginia Smith

Cozy mystery

At the church potluck, Jackie Hoffner's casserole *killed*—literally, unfortunately for the late Mrs. Farmer. Caught in the police searchlights, Jackie would have to rely on handsome Trooper Dennis Walsh and some snooping church ladies to uncover who had cooked up the scheme to frame her.

CAUGHT REDHANDED by Gayle Roper

When Merry Kramer discovered a body while on her morning jog, she wondered whether danger would ever stop following her. She thought she knew the killer, but if she was unable to *prove* what she had found out, was it worth risking her life or losing her wonderful fiancé?

HIDE IN PLAIN SIGHT by Marta Perry

The Three Sisters Inn

The Amish countryside may have been a peaceful escape to craftsman Cal Burke, but returning city girl Andrea Hampton felt only its bitter memories. Family secrets, once bound tight, began unraveling with an attack on her sister and with the neighbors' new hostility. Relying on Cal, Andrea had to get to the truth quickly—her life depended on it.

SCARED TO DEATH by Debby Giusti

A frantic call from a dying friend left Kate Murphy embroiled in a sinister black-market deal and in danger of sharing her friend's fate. Widower Nolan Price was full of secrets, but joining forces with the single father was Kate's only hope to survive.

LISCNM0707